I0543626

Z FOR ZANTO

JaYNe LyoNS

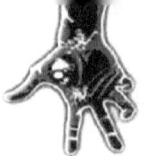

ISBN: 978-1-925952-31-5
Published by Vivid Publishing
A division of Fontaine Publishing Group
P.O. Box 948, Fremantle
Western Australia 6959
www.vividpublishing.com.au

A catalogue record for this
book is available from the
National Library of Australia

ACKNOWLEDGEMENTS

From *the author*

I hope you enjoy reading *Z for Zanto* as much as I did writing it. I love zombie stories and sport – so what better than zombie mayhem on a footie pitch? And the great thing is, that all proceeds of this book go to the wonderful charity - *Save The Children.* So, if you enjoy it – tell all your friends!

Thank you

I'd like to thank my agent Debbie Golvan of Golvan Arts Management, for her time, support and invaluable advice. And many thanks to Anna Hennessy, who created and donated the cover illustration.

From *Save the Children*

Save the Children Australia is one of the World's largest aid and development organisations. We do exactly what our name says – save children's lives.

We go to the toughest places in the world to help children devasted by disasters, disease or conflicts. Our programs improve the health of children, so they survive the critical early years of life to grow up healthy and strong. We believe the best path out of poverty starts in the classroom, so we have programs that create greater access to quality education for all boys and girls. We work to prevent children from being exposed to abuse, neglect, exploitation and violence.

When disaster strikes and children are displaced from their homes, we give them the care and support they need, so they can continue to learn and maintain a normal life, while their communities re-build or they are re-settled.

By supporting *Save the Children*, you are making a real difference to the lives of millions of children – now and in the future.

Thank you

Andrew Chapman, Merchant Group – for seed funding this project, armed only with the briefest of concept briefs, and a good heart.

Woodside Energy – The benchmark in Corporate Social Investment partners. Your vision, passion for rewarding best practise collaboration, and courage to do things differently, sets you apart.

Jayne Lyons – For asking how you could help - and meaning it. For taking the time to understand our work, and the plight of many millions of vulnerable children around the world. And for writing a brilliantly funny book that will not only bring joy and laughter to its readers, it will make them think, empathise and hopefully, act.

ZOMBiE

Life's not easy when you're a zombie, and it's your dream to play soccer. *Especially* when Il Presido's just announced the Hope Games will be in the Capital City, and they're looking for the best players to represent the United Republic Boys. If I wasn't locked up in this awful prison on the Island, perhaps I'd have a shot at the team. But who am I kidding? I'd never get picked now anyway. Everyone thinks that just because you've been dead once, you can't run or pass but only stumble along, dragging your rotting leg behind you. Not that I have a rotting leg by the way, but no one bothers to notice that. Oh yeah, people think you can dribble, but only the *slobber* kind, not the cool Reygo kind.

He's my hero by the way: Reygo, *'The King of Soccer'*. Oh yeah, even zombies have heroes. He's the captain of my team, Real Magique—they play in La Primo League in

Northland. Reygo won the Golden Ball for world's best player for the past three years. It's my dream to play for Real Magique one day too, in the Gladiatorum. At least, that used to be my dream when I was first alive.

But what's the point of having a dream now? Because no one wants a kid with *green skin* on the team, do they? People don't even think of us as human. Guess they hate us, or are scared of us, *or both*. Same difference to me: bolted behind steel gates forever—no freedom—no future—no soccer—no Hope Games. It's not fair.

I know what you're thinking. Zombies are dangerous—they kill people. It's a good job you're all locked up! But not all zombies are bad. We aren't *all* the enemy.

Well, yeah okay, *some* zombies did go mad and do eat people. But that's not all of us. *I've* never eaten anyone, not even a quick bite when no one was looking. I was always a vegetarian—just never liked the taste of meat, and certainly not people. And we don't *all* go around groaning and snarling either. Some of us, the "*Awoken*", came back to life. But no one will bother to listen to or meet us, to see what we're actually like—that we can think and speak again. They don't let us explain that we've done nothing wrong, other than have to leave our home because it was bombed. No. They just put us all on the Island, in a prison, and lock the gates.

Jack says we should be grateful we weren't neutralised,

or sent to the Iron City, because that's what they did to the grown-up zombies. Guess he's right. But it's hard to be grateful for being in this dump.

I can see the soccer pitch through the fence, and it drives me mad to watch the local boys from the Island practising, desperate to be selected for the Hope Games. I dream all day of playing soccer—it's all I ever wanted to do: score goals, just like Reygo. He'll be at the Hope Games, as Goodwill Ambassador. But I'll never get to play, never get to meet him. I'm stuck here in prison forever, or until I die again—*for real* next time. There's no hope for me now.

But you don't even know who I am. My name is Zanto Nero, but most people call me Zero. You can thank my rotten (*rotting*) brother Romeo for that. It was my first day in Infant School, and the new kids were in front of the assembly. We all had to stand up and hold up a big piece of card with our initial. Everyone had to say what their name was, and then they got a clap. It was my turn.

'And what does "Z" stand for Mr Nero?' The teacher asked me.

'Zero!' Romeo called out from the back of the hall before I could reply.

All the big kids laughed, and the teacher wrote it down. I wanted to tell them all that Z was for Zanto, but it stuck, and I was a Zero from then on. And I never got a clap. The only one that still called me Zanto was my dad. That was all in the days before the Infection.

But wait, you don't know about the outbreak, or why I'm on the Island, or why we need a Hope Games. I'd better go back right to the start, to where I grew up—the Shambles.

I bet you know a place like the Shambles. It's that district that's never in the swanky part of a city or town, but perhaps on the outskirts, or in a forgotten quarter near closed down and ruined factories, or maybe where the desert or swamp invades. It's the part of your town nobody chooses to live in if they can afford not to. It's where the poorest folk live—people like me and my friends.

Some families, like mine, live in real houses, but most build their own from old bits of wood, sheets of plastic, or corrugated metal that they scavenge. If you are a rich kid whose parents have a fancy car, then you'd never drive through the Shambles. You'd be scared all the locals are thieves or muggers. Some of them are, and there are some gangsters and alleys you have to avoid. Just like *some* zombies eat people. But if you're from the Shambles, you know that most people are good, or try to be. If you visited us, you'd see how we care for each other and look out for our neighbours—no matter what.

My town is gone now. It's been bombed flat, and

everything I used to know has been destroyed. Still, it wasn't the worst place to grow up, and it's the best place to begin my story.

The Shambles was on the edge of the Iron City, in a big bowl of land surrounded by cliffs on three sides. There was only one main road in or out of our township, through the South Gate. In the distance, you could see the towers and chimneys of the city. It was my home, and I was happy there. It was exactly one year ago when I last saw it. I'm thirteen now, but I was twelve when my story began.

1

ROMEO

The night the world changed seemed just like any other. My brother Romeo was sitting on the couch watching TV, with a beer in his hand—just like he always did when Dad was away. Dad had gone to Capital City in the Third State to see his sister, and Romeo had been lazing in front of the TV for three days straight. I'd yelled at him for not helping in the house or yard, but I didn't dare go nearer, because if he was drinking, he'd likely hit me. He was nineteen then, seven years older than me, and *much* bigger. We were supposed to keep the place straight for Dad, but Romeo was just born idle, I guess. If I tried to get him to help, he'd only snarl at me and stay put. So, I'd leave him and stay in the kitchen.

I knew he wouldn't dare behave like that if Dad was around. Dad yelled at him and told him to find a job, or go back to school. Don't blame my Dad for shouting because he worked so hard for us.

Everyone in our neighbourhood respected him. When I walked past, I'd hear people say, '*That's Denis's boy. A good boy.*' And I'd feel proud, because of the way they said it. Like I was worth something because of *him*, my Dad.

'Suck-up,' Romeo would say and give me a kick.

But I didn't care what he thought. He'd always hated me. Said it was my fault that mum died when I was born. Romeo was always angry. It was best not to annoy him.

Dad was due back that night, and I was waiting up for him. It was a long drive from the Third State. It was eleven pm, and I was sitting at the kitchen table, trying to do my maths homework but really struggling. I was under the electric bulb that hung on a wire. The door was open onto our tiny yard as it was hot and we couldn't afford air-conditioning. Moths and bugs kept bashing into the light, and I could hear the cicadas outside.

I was wearing my red *7 Reygo* replica kit. My backpack was on the table in front of me, and I saw my football boots poking out. They reminded me that if I finished my homework, soccer would be my reward. I went back to my books.

The power gave out and the room went black. It happened all the time—something about the government not having enough fuel. Everything was deathly quiet for a moment, even the cicadas stopped chirruping. Then, my brother gave a kind of snarl, *or roar*? It sounded like someone had stabbed him with a sharp stick. But I guessed it was because his TV had gone blank. It didn't take much to make him angry.

'Romeo?' I called through the door.

He just snarled again. I peeped my head in the door and could just make out that he was trying to get up, but he kept sinking back down in the couch as if his legs wouldn't work. After all, he hadn't moved in three days.

'Are you drunk again?' I demanded.

'Naarrrggg,' he said.

'Yeah, right. I know you are.' He got on my nerves so badly. 'You'd better sober up before Dad gets home,' I warned him, 'or he'll really get mad.'

'Naarrrggg,' the loser repeated.

I'd had enough of him. I didn't care that he'd beat me up. I was furious, for Dad's sake, and determined to teach Romeo a lesson. He was a parasite, like a tick or a leech, sucking all the life out of Dad and giving nothing back. He should've found a good job and taken care of his old man! When I was a professional soccer player, I'd see that Dad was looked after.

I took my metal torch out of my pocket. It was beautiful, like a silver torpedo—small, and powerful. Dad had given it to me for my twelfth birthday. It made me sick to think how many hours he must have worked to save for it. I'd wanted him to take it back to the shop, but he said that I had to keep it, that I was worth it. It was a reward for trying so hard in my exams.

'But Dad, I failed them,' I reminded him.

'But you work hard, and you try to be your best, Zanto,' he said. 'That's why I'm proud of you every day.'

I loved my dad, and I loved my torch. I carried it with me everywhere. I used it now to find my way out into the yard.

Outside, I filled a bucket with cold water. I charged back into the sitting room and dumped the cold water over Romeo. He roared and spat with rage.

'Yeah, well, you shouldn't be sitting on your lazy backside all day, drinking Dad's money,' I yelled at him. 'Get a job, and help around the place for once, you useless…'

My torch shone on my brother's furious face… that is, my brother's furious green face… that is, his boil-covered green face and his bloodshot red eyes and… I took a backward step, as I saw yellow fangs!

Romeo seemed a lot angrier than usual. His red eyes were glaring at me, his mouth slobbering, and his weirdly grown and sharpened teeth were biting up and down as he reached out for me. His fingernails had also morphed into long claws and were black and twisted. I saw a wound on his arm, like a bite mark, which was infested with wriggling maggots. And that's when I noticed the stench. It was much worse than Romeo's normal toxic farts, bad breath, and putrid feet. I knew that smell. I'd once found a dead dog, half-eaten, on the side of the road, out near the desert. It smelt just like my brother—decaying rancid flesh.

'Naarrrggg,' Romeo screamed again and tried to lurch out of the couch.

I took another step back, not able to conjure up a single thought to explain any of this. I'd seen my brother with a hangover before, but this was something *much* worse.

'Grr-wwwwrrr-asghh-ah.'

I yelped and jumped back as Romeo leapt from the couch. I jumped away and fell onto my backside. He grabbed my foot and pulled me towards him. His jaws opened wide showing huge fangs, dripping spit. He was in some sort of weird trance.

'Romeo. Wake up!' I yelled.

I tried to wriggle free, but he was much bigger and stronger than me. He kept pulling me closer. I kicked at his hand.

'Romeo. What's the matter? Stop—please!'

I was desperate, terrified. I tried to kick him again, but I bounced off him like bugs off the electric light. I couldn't escape. He was going to bite me. His mouth opened, and he took a huge bite of my… *shoe*. While he gnawed on the rubber, I managed to release the lace and yank my foot out. I jumped to my feet and backed away to the door. Romeo let out a screech of fury and chased after me on all fours like a manic gorilla.

I raced into the kitchen, grabbing my backpack on the way, and ran out into the yard. Romeo scrambled after me but fell as he left the house—his legs weren't working properly. I leapt over the back fence. He was slavering and gurgling as he chased after me. I landed in the alley as he bashed against the wood.

'Romeo, you need to calm down and sober up before Dad gets home,' I told him through the fence. 'Take some aspirin—you're not well.'

Bam!

I jumped back as Romeo's head bashed through the wooden fence, his eyes insane and his teeth reaching for me, dripping with spit. I bent toward him.

'Seriously dude, *calm down!*' I told him. 'It's okay. I'll do your chores for you.'

Then the wood began to split—he was breaking through.

2

NALA

'*Arrrchhhooo-gggnng,*'

Oh, no way! Romeo, the rotten creep, sneezed all over me, and I was covered in his foul-smelling green spit and snot. I ran to a tap across the alley and washed his slime off. I raced away in my one remaining shoe into the black night, my torch still gripped tight in one hand and backpack over my shoulder.

I ran onto the main road and came to a halt because I could hear others in the dark, snarling, and grunting just like Romeo. I could smell them too, all around, like decaying death. I didn't know what they were, or how many, but they were coming closer. And if they were anything like as angry as my brother, then I didn't want to meet them. I kept moving.

I sprinted for about ten minutes, as if I was racing towards an open goal, but with no idea of direction. I could hardly breathe. I stopped in the middle of the road, my throat raw, trying to catch my breath. I stood with no idea where to go, frozen. I shone my torch, and that's when I heard her voice.

'Zanto—this way.'

Nobody called me Zanto. I was *Zero*. I saw a sliver of light from a crack in a doorway. I stayed where I was. We lived in a dangerous neighbourhood—it could be a trap.

'Who are you?' I hissed.

'Come here. It's safe. Zanto, quick, she's coming back.'

'Who is?'

'Mrs Goodwill—quick. She'll kill you. She's already taken out two others.'

'Huh?'

Mrs Goodwill was tiny, ancient, and as nice as her name sounded. Since when would I be scared of her? I heard a noise behind me and flashed my light.

'Argg!' I leapt back.

Before me was a green and terrifying version of Mrs Goodwill. She was walking with a stick, her handbag over her arm, like a normal old lady. Only, she was snarling with red furious eyes and crooked yellow fangs, just like Romeo. She seemed slow and unsteady, but then she hurled her stick down and flew at me. Her gnarled and bony hands gripped my arms and her teeth sought my neck. I didn't want to be bitten, and I didn't want to hurt a tiny and frail old lady. But that *tiny and frail* old lady's weirdly strong fingers were almost cutting into me, and her fangs were getting closer.

I prised her hands off and pushed her. She fell backwards onto the hard road. But then I did, too, and dropped my torch. It went out. I couldn't see anything, but I could hear and smell Mrs Goodwill searching for me in the dark. She was gibbering and slavering, her claws scratching wildly on the dirt road. My heart was thumping hard, and the skin on my head felt as if it were shrinking. I had no idea why this was happening. All I knew for certain was this crazy old lady was about to tear my throat out.

'Zanto, quick! Come now,' the girl behind me shouted again.

But I couldn't leave my torch. I kept searching. My hand touched shrivelled knobbly fingers—they were icy. The old woman screeched, gurgled, and moved towards me. I jumped back, and my hand found a cold metal cylinder. I turned the torch on.

'Argg!'

The Mrs Goodwill *thing* was right in front of me. She screeched, her red eyes furious, and her mouth stretched wide in a scream as she held her hands in front of the light. I could smell her foul breath. It was like she had digested rotting fish guts and pig livers for a month and then thrown them up. She was one very annoyed, supernaturally tough, mad, and flesh-hungry old lady.

'Quick, Zanto. She doesn't like the light. It hurts her eyes.' The door behind me was open, and a girl was standing there. She beckoned me in. 'What are you waiting for?'

I jumped and raced to the door. The instant the torchlight left the old lady creature, she hurled herself after me. I just made it inside, then turned and slammed the door shut. It was heavy and strong with big metal straps. The girl shot three bolts and stood back.

'You'll be safe in here,' she said.

I stood back and shone my torch on her. She was shorter than me, skinny with black skin and black hair in long braids. She wore glasses and seemed about my age. She looked scared but brave too. She made my memory itchy. I looked around.

We were in some strange place. It was like a shop, only filled with all sorts of junk, like old TVs, radios, books, vases, statues, a stuffed dog, a tricycle, and… well, anything you could think of. There were watches, phones, play-stations, jewelled rings, gold necklaces, and brooches—all kept in glass cabinets behind a wire cage. Strong metal shutters covered the windows. This place was built to keep those inside safe and intruders out. I turned back to the skinny girl.

'So, who are you? How do you know me? Where am I? And what's going on?' I asked.

Outside, Mrs Goodwill screeched and hammered on the door.

'I know you because I've been on the same minibus as you every morning and night for the past year.'

'You have not!'

'I have.'

To get to school every day, I had to get two mini-buses each way, packed with other kids heading for the Iron City. We were the lucky ones whose parents had somehow found a way to send us to the better schools. I thought of my friends sitting at the back of the bus: Ahmed, Mamadou, and Jack. I knew the annoying girls who sat in front of us, always singing, giggling, and whispering. But I couldn't remember ever seeing this one.

'You go to the MSC,' she said (meaning the Metro Sports College). 'And I've seen you play soccer against us at the Academy. You won.'

'Of course, we won. We always win because I *always* score.' I held up my fist and grinned at my triumph against the swot kids. It had been so easy.

'Yeah, I kinda guessed that you loved yourself,' she said.

That made me angry. I glared at her. So, *she* went to the Elite Academy then. The only kids from the Shambles who could go there had to be *really* clever, because you had to get a scholarship and because our folk couldn't afford the fees. I'd never liked the smart kids like her, like Romeo. They always thought I was dumb. I had to make it clear I was better than her, even if she was cleverer than me.

'I'm the best footballer in the whole school,' I said. 'That's not me loving myself—just a fact. I'm going to be as famous as Reygo one day.'

'Who's Reygo?' she asked.

'*Who's Reygo?*' I repeated in disbelief. Was she serious? I pointed at the replica football shirt I was wearing. 'The best player the world has ever known.'

'Player of what?'

What a stupid question. I looked around and caught a glimpse of my face in the mirror—wild black hair covered in dirt, manic dark eyes, a wrinkled-up nose, and a freaked-out look of total disbelief and confusion. Sorry to say, I did not look cool. And anyone who wants to be Reygo must always look cool.

'He plays *soccer*,' I said, smoothing my hair back to Reygo perfection and rubbing off the dirt.

'Oh,' she shrugged. 'I prefer UFC. I'm in training.'

'Yeah, right…' I looked at her skinny arms and gangly legs. *As if.*

We stood there lamely for a minute while the deranged, fanged old lady outside scraped her claws down the door, banging and slobbering. The Mrs Goodwill creature let out a scream that made me jump back.

'She can't get in,' the girl said. 'I knew that you'd never noticed me. My name's Nala, and this is Gran's shop on West Street.'

West Street? That meant I'd run a long way—right to the edge of the Shambles.

'So, where's your Gran?' I asked her.

'She's upstairs, poorly. I was with her when I looked out the window. I saw Mrs Goodwill attack two people and eat bits off them. I called the police, but they didn't answer. Then it got dark and I saw your light, so I came down to help you. I don't know what's happening to the people.'

'My brother tried to eat my foot,' I told her. 'And he was all green, like the old lady—same eyes and sharp teeth. I don't know what's going on either. Where are your mum and dad?'

'They died in a car crash three years ago,' she said.

She sounded sad. I didn't know what to say.

Suddenly, the lights came on. I switched my torch off and looked at Nala. We smiled. In a room behind us, the TV pinged into life. There was a spyhole in the front door. I looked out and saw old Mrs Goodwill screeching angrily at the now bright streetlights. Six others like her appeared on the street, lurching out of doorways, staggering down the road, also shrieking and hissing at the beams.

At least the old woman seemed to have given up on *us*, for she started to hobble towards the others. In fact, they were all walking and limping into a mad scrum. They gathered under the lights, bumping into each other, snarling and hissing as if they had met for some strange kind of Sunday chat.

'Too weird,' I said.

Something was very wrong in the Shambles, only I didn't realise then that it was the end of our world.

3

THE INFECTION

'Zanto—come and see this,' Nala called from the other room.

I walked into the kitchen, and the TV News was on. It showed scenes exactly like the one I'd just seen in the street. Sick, angry people stumbling into swarming groups, yelling and snarling at each other and the lights.

'No-one knows what's wrong with the people, or why they suddenly seem to hate everyone, but it's happening all over the Second State,' Nala said, 'in the Iron City too.'

That's when I thought of Dad trying to come home. Until that moment, I'd been too busy avoiding being eaten by my brother and Mrs Goodwill to worry about him. I searched my backpack for my mobile.

'Oh, no. My phone's at home!' I realised. It had been recharging.

How could I contact Dad and know that he was safe?

'The network's dead anyway,' Nala told me.

I stood next to her and watched the news. The scenes kept changing to random bunches of screeching and snarling green people, bumping into and then away from each other. It was like they were joined with giant invisible elastic bands. We saw police and soldiers try to herd them up, like farmers using dogs to gather sheep. Sometimes the sick people would charge at officers, trying to bite them. Police fired on them with huge water cannons that made them fall over. One of the mad people managed to run right up to a police lady who raised her gun.

We didn't see what happened next because the TV stopped working again. Nala switched on the radio.

'*The government is trying to understand the nature and cause of The Infection,*' the voice said. '*It seems that most of the ill are harmless and confused. However, some are dangerous and will kill. A bite will* **certainly** *infect you...*'

I wondered if that was how Romeo had been infected, through that bite on his arm.

'*...but the virus is also spreading in other ways we don't understand. It seems that the infected are dead—they have no heartbeat.*'

'No way,' I said. I heard my voice like a croak.

Any Infected who can be rounded up safely will be taken to a place of sanctuary and cared for until they recover. However, Il Presido has authorised the army to neutralise any Infected that appear dangerous.

'People must stay indoors and listen to the radio for advice. Anyone on the streets will be assumed to have the virus, so be warned: stay at home and stay safe! If anyone falls sick and their skin begins to look green or their teeth grow, they must call this emergency number...'

The radio crackled and died.

Nala seemed as scared as I felt. We looked out from the shutters at the growling people outside.

'How can they be dead?' she asked.

'I know what this is,' I said. 'Jack said it was going to happen one day. He was prepared. His mum built a wall.'

'What is it?'

'*A Zombie Apocalypse.*'

'Fantastic! So, what do we do now?'

My stomach snarled. I was starving. I was always starving, even if the world was ending.

'Eat something?' I suggested.

We went into kitchen and turned off the lights in case the screeching dead folk outside were attracted to them. Instead, we lit a candle. It was weird that they couldn't keep away from the light, even though it obviously hurt them. They were all still out there, roaring at the street-lights and bouncing into each other like robot toys.

I was on my third peanut butter sandwich.

'Do you like the MSC?' Nala asked.

'I *love* it,' I said and spat a bit of food across the table. 'Sorry.' I wiped it up. 'Except the schoolwork. But if I do that, then I get to play sports every day. I'm way the best at that.'

'I love schoolwork,' she said.

'That's so weird,' I told her.

'No, it's not.'

'Is.'

'Isn't.'

'*Whatever.*'

Well it *was* weird to me. I was useless at schoolwork. But on the soccer pitch: *that* was where I felt like a genius. I loved running with the ball and could outrun anyone. It was like the world was in slow motion, and I could only see the goal.

'And Zanto Nero has come on for Real Magique, replacing his hero, the injured Reygo. Now Zanto is running back for the ball... Oh my, he's stolen it right from under the defend-er's nose, and now he's flying back up the field! The opposition are throwing themselves at him, but he's just side-stepping

them. A skip, a fake, and he's running up the wing. He makes them look like donkeys. He jumps over the fouls, fools the midfielders. I've never seen skill like this.

'He's looking up. He sees the goal. The ball is flying through the air, and the keeper has no chance. He's just standing with his mouth open watching the ball zoom over his head and arc down to the net for a...

'Gooooaaaallllaaaa-Gooooaaaallllaaaa-Gooooaaaalll-laaaa!!!

'Zanto Nero is the hero—he has won the Cuppa. And here comes Reygo limping onto the pitch to congratulate the lad. He picks him up and...'

'Zanto Nero is the best footballer on the planet!' I cried.

'Erm...hello?' Nala's voice interrupted my dream.

I realised I was standing on a chair, my fist in the air, still holding my sandwich. It was deeply uncool. I knew I could get carried away sometimes. I sat back down.

'So, you want to be a footballer,' Nala smiled.

'Maybe, who cares?' I shrugged.

'You're funny,' she laughed.

I hadn't meant to be. Was she laughing at me? How dare she? I was captain of the under 16s team, and I was only 12! Everyone looked up to me. Who was she? I scowled at her.

'I'm going to be a doctor,' she told me.

'Who asked?' I drank some milk.

She frowned at me and we went quiet. I knew I was being mean, but she'd made me feel like an idiot. And what she'd said made me think of my dad again.

Dad was clever like Nala. He read books from the library all the time. When he was little, he'd wanted to be a doctor too, but he'd been too poor to stay on at school. Instead, he started his own business, gardening. He was never bitter.

He would say, 'That's just what life is, Zanto—some things I couldn't fight. I found a better dream, which was to be a good father.'

And that's just how great my dad was. He didn't get to say things on the TV, or in Church, and was never grand like Il Presido, but he'd always say things that made me feel like a hero. He was always there for me. He'd make sure my kit was ready every Saturday, and he'd stand on the sidelines and cheer me on in all weather. When I played great, he would clap; and when I was having a bad day, he'd cheer even louder.

'Work hard, Zanto,' he'd say to me. 'Never give up, and you can be whatever you want to be.'

I loved Reygo, but I loved my dad more.

He worked such long hours every day, whether the sun was scorching, the rain was torrential, or the ground was icy. He'd drive his pick-up truck out of the Shambles to the gardens of the rich folk. Then at night, he worked in a bar so that he could save enough to buy Romeo's schoolbooks, for the Elite Academy, and my new football boots.

Before he was a green slavering dead thing that tried to eat my foot, my brother was clever. Although he had gone to the same infant school in the Shambles as I had, for High School, he'd won a scholarship to the Elite Academy, like Nala. Only he was stupid too. He'd had the brains to be whatever he wanted, but all he did was drop out, drink beer, and watch TV.

Romeo called me *'a retard'*, a Zero. He told Dad he shouldn't waste his time or money on me. But Dad said I was the one who had the drive to achieve my dreams and escape the Shambles, and that Romeo should see me as a role model. My brother hadn't liked that. And to be honest, Dad was the only role model in our family. He always looked out for me. I was determined to be a professional footballer and earn a gazillion dollars, so I could look after Dad and build him a house with a garden of his very own. Only now, I didn't even know where he was or if he was safe. He was going to be so upset by what had happened to Romeo.

'I guess my brother must be dead if he's a zombie,' I said to Nala.

'Sorry about that,' she replied. 'Will you miss him?'

'Suppose so…'

I wouldn't miss doing his chores and getting belted by him.

'I've got to go back home,' I told her. 'My dad will go there looking for me.'

'But it's not safe,' Nala said. 'Not just the zombies, but the army might neutralise you by mistake.'

I didn't actually know what *neutralising* was, but it didn't sound like too much fun. But what else could I do?

'I have to. I'll go as soon as it's light. I need to get my phone, in case Dad can call. He'll be worried.'

'Then I'll come with you,' Nala said. 'We need to stay together.' She was jutting her chin out a bit. She talked tough for a skinny girl.

'I'll be running fast,' I told her. 'You'll never keep up.'

'Oh, I can keep up,' she smiled. 'You sleep on the couch. I'll check on Gran.'

4

BATTLE READY

I thought I'd never sleep, with the world ending outside, my brother a dead flesh-eating zombie, and my dad missing. But I must have passed out with exhaustion, because I woke up on the sofa in the pale light of early morning. Nala was in the kitchen. I looked out through the shutters. The zombies had gone.

'Now's my chance,' I said. 'I'll go and see if Dad's home. If he isn't, I'll leave him a message. You still okay to come?'

'Sure,' she said. She was brave for a girl. 'But we need protection. Come in here.'

We walked into the shop room and looked through the strange junk. Nala created a random outfit. She dressed in an NFL helmet with a grill at the front, a pair of tall riding boots, and a hideous pink leather jacket that came to her bum.

'You look like a *total girl!*' I scoffed.

'Good. Because I am a total girl.' She looked at me through her grill. 'And I fight like a total girl too—a total UFC *champion* girl.'

'Yeah, right.'

I found a motor-biker's padded jacket, a helmet with a visor, and work boots. I looked at myself in the mirror.

'Pretty cool,' I decided. 'But what mad sort of shop is this?' I asked.

Nala looked at me strangely and didn't reply for a while.

'It's a pawn shop,' she said, at last. 'People leave stuff here, and I—I mean *Gran*—lends them money until they can pay it back.'

'You mean you're a…'

She glared at me, her face behind the iron bars daring me to say the word—*Leech*.

I didn't say it.

That's what folk in the Shambles called pawnbrokers. They say they take advantage of poor folk and grow rich off their misery like those parasites suck blood. Dad said that perhaps some pawnbrokers were mean and did exploit folk, but others had a good heart, like anyone else. He said there were good and bad people of every size, colour, creed, and profession, and you could never predict one from the other. He said, even if you met each person and talked to them face to face, you shouldn't ever assume the make-up of their heart and soul—because you could never know for sure. You could only judge someone by their actions. I knew Dad was the exception though—he always thought the best of people. Not many others would walk or talk with a "*Leech*".

I realised then that I did remember Nala—that itchy nag in my memory. The girl no one would sit with on the front seat, who had no friends, because of what her family was. The girl the bullies called names and spat at. The girl who kept her face behind a book all the time, so no one would notice her. And so, I hadn't noticed her—at least not much besides that itchy memory.

I looked around the place. Apart from the few watches and bits of jewellery, it was mostly full of broken old junk. Perhaps Nala and her Gran struggled a bit less than other folk in the Shambles, but they didn't seem to be getting rich off the backs of anyone. Nala looked like a regular girl to me. She was staring at me, like she thought I would spit on her now, like the other kids. But I knew how Dad would expect me to behave. I smiled.

'No worries,' I said. 'Okay, we'll need weapons, in case they attack.'

Nala grinned and nodded. It seemed like we could be friends. She picked up a pool cue and twirled it around fast, first over her head, and then by her side and across her front.

'Ha!' She jumped forward and lunged the stick at me. She stopped just short of my nose by 1 cm. I jumped a bit.

'I learned that in mixed martial arts,' she said. 'Here take this.'

She handed me a baseball bat. I weighed and swung it. It felt good, but then I saw something behind the wire cage doors—a powerful catapult, made of metal and wood. It was around twenty centimetres tall, and its handle was carved like a grinning skeleton.

'Oh, we need that,' I said. 'It's wicked!'

'Ooohh…' Nala screwed up her face. 'I don't think that's a good idea.'

'We need cool weapons, I mean *good* weapons,' I told her. 'Have you got anything better?'

'No, but its owner will be angry if it's not here. He's due to pay the money tomorrow and take it back.'

'He'll never find out if we just borrow it. And even if he does, is it worse than being attacked by a zombie hoard and *not* having a catapult?'

'It might be,' Nala nodded, her eyes big.

'Who can be *that* scary?' I laughed.

'S-Man,' she replied.

I stopped laughing.

S-Man was one of the guys working for Gangster Numero Uno. Romeo hung with him sometimes—that was why he went wrong. Nala was right to be scared. S-Man was bad, bad news.

'I don't know what the S stands for,' she said.

'Psycho,' I told her.

'But that starts with a P,' she pointed out.

'Yeah, *I* know—but he's too dense to realise, and no one's been suicidal enough to tell him. Anyway, he's got '*S-MAN*' tattooed on his forehead, hasn't he? It's too late for a spell-check now.'

Nala laughed. I looked out the window. The sun was now bright and the road still empty. We had to go while we could.

'Okay, I admit that S-Man is as scary as flesh-eating zombies, but we need weapons. I'll tell him I took it. He's a mate of my brother's—it might be all right. Besides, he might already be dead and green too.'

'No other choice, I guess,' Nala nodded. 'You need to find your dad, and we need wicked weapons.'

'Dead right. Let's go then.'

'Don't you need to tell your gran where you're going?'

'No, I don't want her to worry.' Nala said.

"Will she be alright on her own?'

'Oh yeah, as long as we aren't gone too long,' she said. She didn't look at me, but the floor.

'Is everything okay?' I asked.

'Sure. Why wouldn't it be? Shall we go?'

Two minutes later, we stood at the front door. I had my backpack on.

'Ready?' I asked her.

'Born ready!' she grinned.

Carefully, and *very quietly*, Nala began to unlock the bolts. I stood with my visor down, catapult tucked in a leather belt, and the baseball bat ready to swing. We nodded to each other. She pulled the door open.

5

ZOMBIE FIGHT

We crept down the alleyways towards my house. We took it in turns to first peep and then walk around corners—remembering all the moves we'd seen on TV shows. My heart was beating fast; but, fortunately, the streets were strangely deserted. I lifted my visor and let my baseball bat drop down.

'I think we're going to be okay,' I whispered to Nala. 'Looks like they've all gone. Perhaps they don't like the daylight? Or perhaps they're tired because they were up all night screaming?'

'Perhaps,' she replied. 'But where are all the *normal* people?'

'Staying indoors, like the radio said?'

'I suppose so. It's your turn,' she nodded at the next corner.

'All under control—watch the master,' I winked at her.

'Idiot,' she smiled.

I held my baseball bat high and ready, pulled down my visor, and inched my head around the wall.

OMG!

My stomach cramped and gagged from the dreadful rotting smell, and the skin on my head felt tight. There were at least twenty of the dead, all standing with their heads down and swaying, green arms hanging useless, as if they were asleep.

'We need to find another way,' I whispered.

'Why?' Nala frowned.

I pointed my head at the corner. She took a look and jumped back quickly, her dark eyes big and wide.

'There're too many,' she nodded. 'Let's try going back down the alley.' She pointed in the direction we had come from. The Shambles was like a maze. There was always another route to where you needed to go.

'Yep.'

We walked back down the way we'd come, a narrow and tall alleyway with rough shanty wood and tin shacks backing onto it. Some folks had rickety doors that opened onto the passage from their huts. We were halfway down when we smelled the dead. There was a bend ahead.

'I have a bad feeling about this,' I whispered to Nala—a Star Wars moment.

'Me too,' she nodded. 'But we can't go back either.'

She twirled her pool cue and nodded at me. I held up my baseball bat.

'Okay,' I mouthed. 'But be very quiet.'

She nodded, and we moved forward, like silent deadly assassins, towards the crook in the alley.

Crash!

I'd been so focussed on what might be around the corner, that I'd walked into a pile of old bottles in crates! They fell over with horrible loud smash. Nala looked at me with disbelief.

'Why?' she mouthed.

'*Sorry…*' I shrugged, trying to climb out from the mess, but making even more noise.

'Gnnarrragggh.'

We heard them snarling, then we heard them shuffling. We stepped backwards down the alley.

'Gnnarrragggh.'

Whoa! Now *that* noise came from behind us! We'd woken up the sleeping zombies we had been trying to sneak away from in the first place.

'Not fair!' I gasped.

'Crap,' Nala swore. Not so much a goody-goody swot after all, then.

They came from both directions, packed into the passage, row after row of them—green-skinned zombies, lurching and limping, red-eyed and yellow-fanged, with hideous talons.

'We're trapped,' Nala said, her pool cue raised and ready.

'Don't give up yet,' I cried and started kicking at a creaking door that led from the passage to a shack. 'Aha —victory!' I managed to knock it down. 'Argg! No way.'

My triumph didn't last long. All I'd done was release another hissing green lady zombie from inside the hut.

She looked like she used to be someone's mum cooking dinner, still with her apron on, and a big wooden spoon in her hand. But, unlike most mums, she flew at me, her talons reaching and fangs dripping. I was too shocked to react, and I couldn't hit a lady. I fell back into the passage with the mad dead woman throwing her arms around me. But hang on—she wasn't trying to *bite* me; she was trying to *feed* me. She was pushing the spoonful of old mouldy green food into my mouth, like I was her baby. Perhaps she was harmless after all. But I wasn't going to take the risk. I spat out the putrid food, but her vile rotten slobber was dripping onto me.

Whack!

Nala's pool cue knocked the dead lady unconscious. Can the dead be unconscious? But, I didn't have time to answer that because...

Wham!

Nala twirled on her toes and kicked the head of the first zombie attacking from the alleyway on the right. Then...

Zham!

She twirled her cue and took out some huge fat undead dude on her left with a sharp knock to his head.

For a second she was frozen in the coolest ultimate warrior pose, and all I could do was stare at her in amazement. This was the scared girl from the front seat that never spoke, right? But then, the hoard started to surge forward from both sides. Perhaps they didn't all want to hurt or eat us; perhaps some others just wanted to feed us with wooden spoons too, but I wasn't waiting to find out.

'Nala—quick!'

I pulled her into the tin shack that the zombie mum had run out from. We had to escape from the alleyways. Once inside, I closed the door, and we pulled down whatever furniture we could against it.

'Hurry up,' I shouted.

The zombies were already breaking through. We ran outside, but I realised that Nala wasn't with me. I turned back. She was struggling with an evil-looking zombie. There was no doubt about him: he was a man-eater. I saw her terrified eyes.

'Zanto, help me!' she cried.

I pulled out S-Man's catapult, picked up a stone from the ground, and took aim. If I'd had more time, I would've been too scared of hitting Nala—instead I let it rip.

Thwack.

The fat zombie fell to the floor. I pulled Nala to her feet, and we ran.

At last, we lost sight and sound of any zombies and were able to relax and drop back to a walk.

'Not bad fighting for a girl,' I nudged Nala.

'Not bad for a boy,' she nudged me back.

'Thanks for saving me,' I said.

'Same,' she smiled.

I felt safe knowing she had my back.

6

GiNGA-NUT

We were almost at my back yard, with no further sight of anyone living or dead, when we were startled by a shout.

'Oi, Zero. I thought you was a gonner for certain!'

It was Jack, sitting on the tin roof of his house. He was dressed in army combats and holding a huge pair of binoculars. His face was painted in green and black camouflage stripes, but it was obvious it was the Ginga-Nut, because of his massive ears and frizzy orange hair. He was holding a souped-up and mega-modified sub-machine *nerf gun*. He climbed over and jumped down on the ground next to us.

'That's so cool,' I said, looking at his gun. 'Can I have a shot?'

'Yeah. Only careful—we've increased the pump pressure by ten times. If it hits you in the eyes, it'll kill you. I took a zombie down at twenty metres yesterday.'

'You wiped out a zombie with foam pellets?' Nala frowned.

'Not *foam*. We've got Ma's secret weapon—her unbreakable biscuit bullets,' G-Nut replied.

'You knock them out with *cookies*?' She laughed. 'As if.'

'Watch this little girl,' he turned and fired.

Bam-bam-bam-bam-bam-bam-bam-bam-bam-bam-bam-bam!

He blasted out the windows of the house opposite like he had a machinegun. It was more powerful than any nerf gun I'd ever seen.

'Whoa,' I cried. 'I've got to have one.'

'What about those people's windows?' Nala said. 'You'll get it now.'

'Don't worry about the Jacksons complaining,' G-Nut pointed at the shattered glass. 'They all turned zombie, and I ran them off down the street with this little devil and Ma's baked bazookas.'

He patted his gun, reached into his pocket, and produced a handful of hard brown ammo. I took one, smelled it, and hammered it on the wall. It was a rock-hard, bullet-shaped cookie.

'Here you go, Zero, check it out,' Jack handed me the gun.

It felt way heavier than a normal nerf as it had an extra lever system on it.

When I pump-loaded the chamber, I could feel the power waiting to be released.

Bam!

I let it rip and another window shattered.

'That's brilliant,' I laughed. 'How did you make it?

'Ma did it—she understands engineering and stuff. Only she's so bad at baking, which was how we discovered how to make the bullets. She wanted us ready for the Apocalypse. Let's go inside.'

Jack's tiny house and yard was surrounded by an eight-foot wall, with barbed wire on top. We went in through a steel-barred gate. I'd done this a hundred times before without thinking anything of it. Two years ago, Jack and his mum had spent every weekend building it out of old bricks they found around the Shambles. They'd been expecting the end of the world.

Jack's mum was in the yard—he didn't have a dad. Mrs P (that's all I'd ever called her) was dressed in combats too. She gave us a slice of mango each. Nala and I took off our helmets. It seemed strange: standing in their yard, being polite, eating fruit, and talking about the Apocalypse. Their phones, TV, and radio weren't working either, and all the electricity had gone off again. But G-Nut and his mum seemed totally calm about it.

'What did you see on look-out Jack-boy?' Mrs P asked.

'The army's building a huge fence, so no more zombies can get in,' Jack replied pointing at the South Gate (that was the only route in or out of the Shambles). 'We'll be safe enough here, once they come and clear the Infected away.'

'Oh yes, we're prepared,' Mrs P confirmed. 'We've built up our supplies.'

We told the story of our last 24 hours, of my brother being a zombie, my escape, Dad being away, and Nala's sick gran. Mrs P went inside to sort some stuff out, but we stayed in the yard.

G-Nut stared at Nala.

'Hey, I know her. She's the freak from the bus,' he said. 'What's she doing with you, Zero? You're the captain of the MSA Under-16s Soccer team. You can't hang with a dirty *Leech*.'

Nala's black eyes narrowed. She began to swing her pool cue like a pendulum.

'Call me a *Leech* again, Dumbass, and see what happens,' she said and stepped forward.

Not happy with wiping out zombies, Nala was now ready to fight with the G-Nut and his nerf-gun. Was this truly the same girl who'd kept her head down when the boys called her worse names than *Leech*, and who the other girls spat on? Seemed like the end of the world for them meant the start of a new one for her.

Jack stepped up.

'Okay, you're a…'

'Whoa, G-Nut, don't be an idiot,' I interrupted him. 'Her name's *Nala*—just call her that. It doesn't matter what her family does, because she's okay. Besides, she's my friend, and you don't call my friend names.'

Jack squared up to me. I was taller, but he was strong, and he had a massive gun. Nala was still swinging her pool cue and looking pretty angry.

'You'd side with a L… with *her*, rather than me, your best mate?' He shook his head. 'Why?'

'Because she saved my life last night. And besides, she's some kick-ass, UFC-trained warrior,' I carried on. 'Those of us left in the Shambles should stick together, not pick on each other.'

Jack glared at me, and at Nala. She gave it back, still looking like she was about to swing her cue at his stupid head. Suddenly, he shrugged.

'Whatever. We've got deader and greener things to worry about. We all cool?' He stepped back.

'I am,' Nala said, and lowered her pool cue. They didn't shake hands, but it was as much as I could hope for.

'So, have you seen my Dad's pick-up, G-Nut?'

'No. Mr Nero didn't come back. But I looked in at your place this morning. Your brother was in the back yard going zombie-crazy because he couldn't get out. You can't go back home, Zero,' Jack said, and put his hand on my shoulder. 'Sorry.'

'Right…' So, was that it? I had to give up all hope for my brother? He may have been the worst brother ever, but he was the only one I had. 'But I have to get my phone and stuff and leave a message for Dad.'

'Okay,' Jack nodded. 'You can write the note here. Are you brave enough to come?' he asked Nala.

'Yeah—are *you*?' Nala snorted at him.

'We're *all* brave enough,' I said.

Nala and I put our helmets back on. Jack came over and put his arm on my shoulder.

'Whoa! How commando do we look?' He posed with his gun.

'You look like a Boy Band,' Nala said and twirled her stick.

'Who asked you?' Jack scowled at her.

'You did, just then. So, are you done posing? Can we go?'

7
BACK HOME

We all ran commando-style down the alley towards my back yard. There was no sign of anyone alive or dead. I imagined all the neighbours huddled inside their tiny houses, safe behind locked doors, not daring to come out, waiting for the TV or radio to come back on and for the government spokespeople to tell them what to do. We reached my back fence. I couldn't hear anything. I peeped inside the hole that Romeo had made with his head.

I could see my zombie brother. He was sitting slumped in the corner, on the hard dirt, his head drooped down, and green spit trailing from his mouth. There were blood and feathers on his face and on the ground nearby, and Dad's chicken coop was empty. Looked like he'd found something to eat. At least it wasn't my foot. He seemed to be sleeping now. It was strange looking at him, knowing he was dead, only not quite. I tried to find one happy memory of us together, but I couldn't. I didn't count his shoving my head down the toilet. Still, I was dreading how poor Dad would feel when he saw him.

Meanwhile, Jack had climbed on the roof of the shack next door. Nala stayed at the fence. The plan was that I'd sneak through the front door, and if they saw Romeo move, Nala would try to distract him at the back fence. If that didn't work, then Jack would knock him out with his nerf machine gun.

'I'm a dead shot—I won't miss,' he promised.

I hoped he was right, because if that didn't work, my only plan B was to run away fast. Jack gave me the thumbs up and had his nerf ready. It was time to go.

'Be quiet, be quick, and be careful,' Nala said to me.

'Okay, yes, and will do,' I nodded at her. Not sure who made *her* the leader though. *I* was the captain of the team.

My heart was pumping like I'd run the full length up a soccer pitch. I sprinted around the corner and up the alleyway that led to the front of the house. I opened the door quietly, and stepped, *very carefully*, forward. I couldn't see, hear, or smell Romeo, so hopefully he was still in the yard digesting the live chicken. I snuck into the kitchen. All clear, but the back door was wide open, and I could smell my brother's rotten stench. I was on full alert. Unlike the mum zombie, Romeo had definitely wanted to eat my flesh. I took out the note I'd written to Dad and put it on the table.

'Whoa. Hey. You there! Hiya!'

I jumped as I heard the loud commotion from outside. It was Nala, shouting and banging on the back-yard fence. Through the window, I saw Romeo lurch forward towards her. He was awake and dangerous. I had to find my mobile phone quick. I was sure it'd been recharging in the kitchen last night while I was doing my homework, but I couldn't see it anywhere. Perhaps it'd been knocked somewhere by Romeo.

I looked out of the window and saw it in the middle of the back yard, still attached to the charger cable. It was right behind Romeo, who was busy snarling at Nala and trying to reach her through the hole in the wall. This would be my only chance. I stepped out into the back yard and looked up at Jack on next-door's roof.

'Are you mad?' he mouthed at me and twirled his finger next to his ear.

I shrugged. Perhaps. But this might be my only hope of ever talking to Dad again.

'Hey, you, Dead-brain. This way!' Nala shouted and whistled.

Romeo snarled, no doubt furious he couldn't eat her. I stepped forward a bit more. Jack was shifting around on the roof, trying for a better aim with his nerf gun. I grabbed my phone. Jack moved his foot and a red tile slid down from the roof and landed with a crash behind me.

'Crap!' Jack swore.

Romeo turned and spotted me.

'Shoot!' Nala yelled up to Jack.

Romeo let out a bellow of anger and charged, red eyes blazing, talons reaching for me.

Bam-bam-bam-bam!

The earth all around us exploded as Ginga-Nut's biscuit bullets missed their mark. So much for him being a great shot. Romeo crouched away from the noise and bullets.

'Sorry, Zero, I was slipping,' Jack shouted. 'I've got more, but I've got to reload.'

Romeo jumped up and glared at me, his red eyes full of fury.

'Whoa—run Zanto, quick!' Nala cried.

I was already running, crashing through the kitchen door. I tried to hold it closed against my brother, my hands braced and feet sliding back over the floor, but he was too strong. I left the door and scrambled across the kitchen. I heard Romeo thunder after me. I was nearly at the front door when...

'Nnaaarggg!'

Too late—he had me.

I rolled onto my back. He was above me, his mouth wide and his teeth sharp, ready to bite. His eyes were full of hatred. Romeo was too strong—I couldn't move. Poor Dad, he was going to come home to find us both zombies. Romeo fell onto my neck. I braced myself for the pain!

And then—and then—and then—nothing! Romeo *started snoring*. What? How? I pushed him off and saw G-Nut standing there, holding his nerf. He'd knocked Romeo out after all.

'He shoots, he scores. Ginga-Nut 1, Romeo 0,' Jack cried, grinning.

I pushed Romeo off me. He lay on his back snoring loudly.

'Thanks, G-Nut,' I high-fived Jack.

While Jack stood guard, I stuffed some clothes into my backpack, and grabbed my Cuppa replica football—I wasn't leaving that behind. I guessed that Romeo had eaten my shoe, so I put on my old sports shoes, which had holes. I found Dad's moneybox, which he kept for emergencies. I took all the money from inside—I knew he wouldn't mind. It was about three thousand dollars, his life savings. Just about enough to buy a new second-hand truck, if ever he needed to. I'd keep it safe until I saw him again.

I stopped above my brother, lying there, snoring.

'Catch you later, Romeo,' I said.

8

STILL ALIVE

Five minutes later, we were safely back in Jack's place. The electricity was on again, and Mrs P was watching TV.

'They've managed to restore transmission, but it won't last long,' she said.

The orange-tanned announcer looked very serious. He was in front of a screen that showed images of the green, dead zombies gathering in groups in the plaza of Iron City.

'*The Iron City and the Second State are infected and under full quarantine...*'

'That's us,' said Nala.

'*The Third State is still safe, and to protect it, no one is allowed to enter without a visa. Anyone alive trying to enter illegally will be sent to prison. Any zombie that enters the Capital City will be neutralised.'*

'What *is* neutralised?' I asked.

'Got rid of forever,' Nala said.

That didn't sound too good.

'We now know that the Shambles is the source of the epidemic, and that everyone there is now infected and dead,' the TV presenter continued.

'No way!' Nala jumped up.

'The township has been sealed off. It's too dangerous for the army to enter. A fence has been erected so that none of the infected can escape. If the fence collapses, measures will be taken to extinguish the threat, for the greater good.'

'That fence is to keep *us* in, not the zombies out!' Jack yelled.

"Measures will be taken to extinguish the threat?" I repeated. 'What does that mean?'

'Nothing good,' Mrs P said.

The TV showed images taken from a helicopter flying over the Shambles. Every scene was of snarling and froth-mouthed green zombies with insane red eyes and yellow fangs. All the healthy living people were hiding indoors, like we'd been told to.

'But we're not all zombies here!' Jack yelled at the TV.

'That fence won't hold out against a zombie hoard,' Mrs P said. 'Something terrible will happen if it falls.

Prepare for Operation Exit, Jack. We have to get out—you know the drill.'

Jack jumped up. 'Yes, Ma!' he saluted.

Then we heard a helicopter overhead. I had an idea. I took off my helmet, and heavy jacket, pulled on my football boots and grabbed my ball. I was still wearing my soccer shirt.

'Come on, quick. We need to look as normal as we can for the camera. Let everyone in the United Republic see that we're just kids, not zombies. Then they'll send help.'

I ran outside into the middle of the dirt road with Nala, and Jack followed with his nerf gun.

The helicopter hovered above us. The *whop-whop-whop* of the blades sent a wind that moved my hair into waves. I saw the black-glass, bug-eyed visors of the soldiers looking down, one of them holding a TV camera.

'Hey look, we're alive,' I waved at them. 'Can a zombie do this?'

I started playing keepy-uppy, kicking the ball up and over my head, onto my back, along my shoulders, and then back to my feet again. Meanwhile, Nala was jumping somersaults and power-kicking like a UFC martial arts champion. Jack was dancing like a robot that needed some oil. Not sure what he thought he was proving. He looked as stiff and lame as any zombie.

'G-Nut, loosen up, dude,' I yelled above the noise. 'Oi, see us!' I called up to the chopper. 'I'm a footballer,' I pointed at my shirt, 'not a zombie.'

Pah Pah Pah Pah.

That was Nala kicking. Now Jack was *moonwalking*. He was rubbish at that too and fell over.

'G-Nut, try to be cool,' I advised him, smoothing my hair back to Reygo perfection again.

'There're still filming us—it must be working,' Nala cried. 'El Presido will tell the army to rescue us.'

The helicopter came a bit lower, as if the soldiers were checking us out. The wind from the blades was so strong, I had to fight to stand straight.

'They can see we're alive,' I laughed in relief.

'Lookout!' Nala cried.

Zombies appeared on all sides—I guess attracted by the sound of the chopper. Nala jumped in front of me with kind of twisting leap while twirling her pool cue, just like the moves you see from Jackie Chan or Jet Li.

Bat—bat—pow.

She knocked three zombies onto their backsides before I could react. She jumped around and faced us.

Whip-klunk.

She thrust her stick past G-Nut and knocked out a zombie mum that was sneaking up behind him. He just stood there like an idiot with his mouth open watching her.

'Zanto, behind you!' she warned.

I saw the creature from the corner of my eye, moving fast. What could I do? I remembered a spectacular Reygo move. I kicked the football high in the air, and then made like I was scoring an overhead scissors goal. Instead, I slammed the zombie onto the floor with my flying foot, completed the somersault, landed on my feet, and then neatly caught the ball. I looked around for the applause. Nothing.

'Oh, come on! That was amazing,' I complained.

There was a green granny charging up behind Nala— Mrs Goodwill again. Her mouth was wide, and her yellow fangs dripped as she shrieked. She was definitely a man-eater. I tossed the ball up.

Wham.

I slammed a perfect volley onto the old woman's head. She bounced off the ball and fell with a puff of dirt onto the floor. Jack fired his nerf gun at another zombie who seemed so shocked at the sting in its backside that it slouched off, looking very sorry for itself, its lower lip wobbling like it might cry. Seems like they felt pain after all. So, then, how could they be completely dead? Nothing made sense.

We stood, all three, back-to-back, breathing hard, surrounded by groaning, and dazed dead folk. They wouldn't stay down for long. I dropped my ball to the floor, put my foot on it, and pulled my shirt to show the camera in the helicopter.

'Not dead yet,' I yelled. 'Tell Il Presido to help us.'

The soldiers looked down. Another zombie, a grown man, charged us.

Zap.

I took him down with my skull catapult.

The helicopter came down, even lower, until it was just above our heads.

'They're going to help us,' Jack shouted above the noise.

But they didn't land. Instead, a voice on a sound system boomed down, above the roar of the blades.

'*Sorry, kids, we can't help you. The Shambles is overrun. We don't have the manpower to clear this township of the dead. Our orders are to leave immediately. We need to stop the Third State from being overrun too. But, we'll report back that you folk are still alive here. See if they can delay the bomb...*'

'Did he say *bomb?*' I turned to the other two. They nodded. 'Whoa, hang on—what *bomb?*' I shouted.

'*The Dead are all heading for the fence over the South Gate,*' the soldier carried on. '*If the barricade breaks, they'll drop a bomb to save the rest of the Republic. The whole Shambles will be destroyed.*'

'But they're not all bad,' I shouted back. 'You can't just bomb them all.' Some of the zombies hadn't wanted to hurt us at all, like the mum who just wanted to feed people. But the soldiers couldn't hear us.

'*Get out, if you can. Go to the north and climb the cliffs. Make for the Third State across the Black Mountain. Good luck, kids. But go quick—we're sorry…*'

'No!' I yelled.

The helicopter flew away, heading north. I couldn't believe they'd just left us and that they might destroy the Shambles with a bomb. All around us, the dazed zombies started to wake up.

'Come on Zanto,' Nala handed me my football. 'We have to go.'

I looked at her. 'Okay,' I agreed.

Back in the house, Mrs P was busy packing bags.

'Oi, Zero—come up here,' G-Nut yelled.

Nala and I trooped outside. Jack was on the roof with binoculars.

'Come see,' he said. 'You won't believe it!'

9

FREE ICE-CREAM

We climbed up and borrowed the binoculars. We were on a hill in the centre of the Shambles, and from that high point on the roof, we could see in all directions. The township was in a bowl of land surrounded by cliffs on three sides. The houses were crammed into the valley and clung onto the slopes until they became too steep. Across the break in the cliffs was the South Gate, where the soldiers had built the massive fence. We saw them finishing the last section. Any zombies that came near them were fired on with a water cannon and they fell over and crawled around in the mud.

We could see all the alleyways and squares from that viewpoint. Zombies all around us were limping and lurching their way south, towards the fence. They looked like lines of ants walking home after finding a hotdog.

'The noise of the construction is attracting them,' Nala said.

'Yeah, and when they all reach the fence,' Jack pointed, 'they'll push it over. Then we get bombed!'

I looked in the opposite direction towards the cliffs. The streets seemed empty. The north path was only one other way out of the Shambles now that the South Gate was blocked. It was a tiny and narrow, made of hundreds of slippery stone steps cut out of the rock. It climbed the cliffs onto the Black Mountain. I could see some people on the steps trying to escape. You certainly couldn't take anything more than a backpack on that route. The soldiers were right—that way was our best hope.

'We'll have to take the cliff path,' I pointed. 'But how will we get your Gran up there?'

'Oh, Gran—yes,' Nala suddenly looked nervous. 'I don't know.'

'Ma knows another way out of the Shambles,' Jack said, lowering his voice to a whisper, even though we were the only ones on the roof. 'But you have to promise not to tell anyone else.'

'Like who?' I looked around.

'Spit promise,' he insisted.

'Okay,' we spat and shook hands.

'There's a secret tunnel that Grandpa showed Ma years ago. She always said we could escape the Shambles in an emergency. Only problem—the entrance is in *Brick Alley*.'

He pointed away from cliff path to the roughest part of town, the place you really didn't want to go to if you could help it.

'Brick Alley? *Brilliant*,' I sighed.

Brick Alley was the worst part of town. That was where GN1, Gangster Numero Uno, hung out. *Numero Uno* didn't mean the best, but the most cruel and dangerous. I could see his flag flying from where we were—black with a white cross on it. It meant keep out if you know what's good for you. And *S-Man* was one of his gang. I looked down at my catapult. I wasn't looking forward to meeting *him* either.

'What choice have we got?' Nala shrugged. 'We have to get out. But I need to go home first.'

'Yeah, you need to get your gran,' I nodded. 'I'll come with you. But we need to be quick. Who knows how long the fence will last?'

'No, that's okay. I can go on my own,' she said. 'I'll meet you guys in Brick Alley.'

'You can't get an old lady out on your own,' I said. 'We need to stick together.'

Nala took off her NFL helmet—she seemed nervous.

'Gran's dead,' she said quietly. 'I lied to you.'

'What? Why?'

'Because that's what I tell everyone. Gran died in hospital in the Iron City three months ago. I ran away before they could ask where I lived. I didn't want anyone to know I was on my own. No one in the Shambles or at my school knows. I tell everyone that she's in bed, sick. I go to school during the day, and then open the shop at night and the weekends.'

'But why not just ask for help?' I asked.

'Because they'd send me to the orphanage in the Iron City. I don't get a full scholarship for the Academy, and I need money to pay part of the school fees. If I can't work in the shop and earn money, I'd have to stop going to school, and I'd never get to be a doctor. Wouldn't you do anything to keep your dream?'

'I wouldn't lie to a mate,' I said.

'I'm sorry,' she replied. 'I know that I can trust you now, Zanto.'

'Why do you want to go back home if the bomb's coming?' I asked.

'To get all my money and stuff if we're leaving. So, are we friends still?'

I stared at her for a while. She did look sad.

'Sure, of course,' I shrugged.

'So, if you two have finished the romantic scene, shall we go?' Jack said.

'Why are you coming?' Nala asked.

'Not for *you*. Zero was my best mate before you showed up, and mates stick together.'

I slapped him on the back.

'Nice one, G-Nut. Let's go.'

'Yeah thanks,' Nala said.

Dressed once more in our protective gear and carrying our weapons, we ran away from the ant-lines of dead folk heading south. Now and then, I saw curtains twitching as we raced past.

'There are people alive here,' Nala pointed.

'Yeah, I see them.'

'Do you think they know about the bomb?' she asked

'How can they? The soldiers only told us.'

'Oh no…' She looked back as we ran.

I knew how she felt—we needed to warn them.

Next minute, mega result, we found an abandoned ice cream van! G-Nut jumped inside the cab. The keys were in the ignition.

'Anyone for ice-cream?' He switched on the engine.

'*La-di-la-di-la-di-la… La-di-la-di-la-di!*' The tinny music blasted out.

'Shush, idiot!' Nala cried. 'Every zombie for miles will come.'

'Whoops,' Jack grimaced. 'No worries, here's the

control,' he flicked off the music speaker, climbed into the back, put on an apron and hat and opened up the windows.

'Now then, what can I get you folks?' He looked ridiculous, in a stripy cap, with his carrot hair sticking out, and camouflaged face grinning.

'Lamebrain,' Nala shook her head. 'We don't have time for messing about.'

I lifted my black visor. 'Double choc swirl, please,' I said.

Nala looked at me through the grill of her helmet.

'Seriously? There's a zombie hoard all around us, and maybe a bomb on the way? This isn't the time for a snack.'

'I'm starving and hot,' I replied. I took off my helmet and dropped my baseball bat.

'Nice one, Zero,' Jack pulled on the levers and created the biggest, most ridiculous ice cream swirl cone I'd ever seen. It was already leaning to one side, ready to fall off.

'Brilliant,' I laughed and took it quick before it collapsed. Jack made himself an even bigger bright blue cone and came outside to us.

'Taste this one Zero—bubble gum flavour,' he pushed it into my face and snatched my chocolate swirl. I took a whopping bite of blue cream.

'Whoa, brain freeze!' I groaned.

'Oi!' G-Nut yelled at me. 'Too much; give it back.'

'There's a truck full of it,' I spurted at him and pointed.

'Whoa, don't spray it!' He laughed and wiped my blue spit off his face. We swopped back again.

'Want a taste?' I offered mine to Nala.

'It looks like a giant, soggy dog poo,' she said.

'Doesn't taste like it,' I said, with a mouthful. 'Go on, try.'

'I'm not into sharing spit,' she said.

'Don't be a girl, go on,' I shoved the ice cream under her nose. I knew she'd give in. It smelled so good. She licked it and smiled.

'Okay, that is good. You're not getting it back!' She started to eat it fast.

'Whoa!' I wrestled it back before she ate it all.

After, we sat in the shade of the truck, three in a row. I was feeling good from the sugar hit.

'This is my favourite bit of the end of the world so far,' I decided.

'Me too,' Nala said, still with chocolate smears round her face.

Jack burped. 'I'm going to throw up,' he said. 'In a good way.'

'Nice,' Nala stood up. 'We'd better go. It's still a long walk to the shop.'

'We don't have to walk, I can drive us,' Jack said.

'As if. Since when?' I looked at him, checked to see

if his big ears were wriggling, a sure sign of him telling ripe ones.

'Ma taught me—said we needed to be ready for the end of the world. Come on then. Let's go.'

He jumped into the cab. Nala and I looked at each other, still not buying it. He switched on the ignition and started the engine. Still expecting a trick, we climbed into the cab. Jack moved the gearstick, revved the accelerator, and we lurched off. Okay, we were going down the road in big jumps, but we were going.

'Nice one, G-Nut,' I held up my hand for a high five.

'The ultimate driver on earth,' Jack grinned and swung his hand for mine. We almost crashed into a wall.

'Whoops…' he managed to get us back on course just in time. 'Sorry.'

'Idiots,' Nala shook her head.

Jack drove the ice-cream van to her place.

10

WARNiNG

'Whoa, look at all this stuff,' G-Nut said as we walked around Nala's shop.

She was filling a bag with bits of jewellery, watches, and money, but leaving most of the valuables behind the locked cage doors.

'Why not take it all?' Jack asked.

'It's not mine,' she said. 'It belongs to the people who left it here. I'm only taking stuff that people told us to keep rather than wait for them to repay their debts.'

'But there might not be anyone alive here in two days,' Jack said. 'Let's take it all.'

'I can't,' Nala shook her head. 'Gran would be angry.'

'But she's not here anymore, is she? *We* need it. It's only going to get bombed. Tell her Zero.'

What would Dad do? I shook my head.

'Nala's right; it's not our stuff,' I said.

'For real?' Jack snorted. 'No way are you two soft losers surviving the Apocalypse.'

'You neither, Lamebrain,' Nala said. 'Even knuckle-draggers will need *one brain cell* in the New World.'

'Burned G-Nut,' I said. 'Come-on, let's go quick.'

We loaded everything into the ice cream van. Nala paused at her front door, her backpack over her pink leather shoulder, and pool cue in the other hand.

'You alright?' I asked her.

'Yeah, just sad, that's all. I've lived here my whole life and now I'm leaving it all behind. It might not even be here tomorrow. And who knows what kind of life we'll have in the Third State.'

'Yeah. The end of the world sucks, I know. But we have to go.'

She nodded, locked the door, pulled on her NFL helmet, and jumped into the ice cream cab. Jack started the engine.

We hadn't gone far when we saw a face at the window of a shack. It was a little kid staring at us. Behind him, his mum appeared, and they looked very scared. Perhaps they'd heard the TV say that the Shambles was overrun and no one was coming to help us. But they didn't know that they had to leave as soon as they could.

'Stop the van. We need to tell them to leave,' Nala said. But Jack kept driving.

'No time,' he said.

'G-Nut stop being an idiot and stop the van,' I yelled.

'Fat crap!' He swore and slammed on the brakes, just avoiding a crash with a clapped old truck approaching on the narrow road. Inside it was a mum and dad, and two little kids. The truck was packed to busting with all their belongings. Jack opened his window.

'Where are you guys headed?' he asked.

'The South Gate,' the dad said and pointed. 'Get out while we can.'

'That's no good,' I said. 'All the zombies are moving down there, you'll never get close. You need to head for the north cliff path.'

'We already tried. It's blocked by the Infected too,' he said.

'So, there's no way out?' the mum asked, her voice shaky. 'Guess we have to go back home and wait for the army to come to save us.'

The three of us in the cab looked at each other.

'The army's not coming,' Nala said. 'You have to escape now, because they're going to drop a bomb here.'

'What can we do?' The mum looked scared and the two kids staring crying. Could I tell them how to escape when I'd made a spit promise with a best mate? But then I knew what Dad would do, promise or no promise.

'Go to Brick Alley,' I said. 'That's the only way out now. There's a tunnel there.'

They all looked terrified. No one went to Brick Alley.

'Shut it, Zero, you idiot!' Jack pressed the button and the window went up. 'You promised not to tell. You spat in my hand.'

'I had to, G-Nut,' I said. 'Else they'll all die.'

'Zanto's right,' Nala said.

'Who asked you, *Leech*?' Jack scowled.

'Watch your mouth, Lamebrain,' Nala cried and tried to whack him with her helmet. I managed to keep them apart.

'Cut it out, G-Nut,' I said.

'So how come *she's* allowed to call me Lamebrain then? She thinks she's better than all of us, just because she goes to the Elite Academy.'

'Okay no more name calling, anyone. You two cool?'

They scowled at each other, but at last, they nodded.

'So, G-Nut, why can't we tell people about the tunnel?' I asked.

'Wise up! Because we have to get through Brick Alley, and Gangster Numero Uno controls it. What if he won't let everyone through? We need to make sure that *we* get away safe.'

'And what about them?' I pointed at the little kid

and his mum, still watching from the window, and the family in their truck.

'You're not a hero, *Zero*! Get real—you can't save *everyone*. We have to look after *us*. The weak ones won't make it anyhow,' Jack shrugged. 'You have to leave people behind to survive.'

'What, like Nala's gran? Leave *her* behind?'

'Erm, actually you don't need to worry about Gran,' Nala reminded me.

'It's an Apocalypse, you idiot!' Jack shouted. 'It's every man for himself now. You don't know nothing.'

'I don't want to know stuff like *that*!' I said. 'We're from the Shambles, G-Nut. Have you forgotten already? We help each other out when we're in trouble. We don't leave people to die.'

'Yeah, and best mates keep promises too,' Jack shook his head. 'It's your funeral man, for real.'

Perhaps he was right, but what would *you* do? What would my dad do? I looked at Nala. What would *she* do? She handed the microphone to me and nodded.

'Tell them all,' she said.

'Useless losers!' Jack scowled.

'*La-di-la-di-la-*...' the music wailed out.

I flicked the switch to the microphone.

Anyone who can hear—listen. The army isn't coming to save you. They're going to drop a bomb to destroy the Infected. If you want to live, you have to leave the Shambles now. The

South Gate and Cliff Path are both blocked by the dead, so head for Brick Alley. There's a tunnel there, which can get you to the Third State. If you stay—there's no hope.'

We made sure that Jack zigzagged every alleyway and though he complained and swore the whole time, we repeated our message over and over. It wouldn't be our fault if people were left behind in the Shambles when the bomb came.

Jack was still furious by the time we got back to his place. And Mrs P wasn't too thrilled either.

'It might a *noble* thing to do Zanto,' she said. 'But now everyone in the Shambles will be heading for Brick Alley, and who knows if we'll even reach the tunnel. We have to go quick, and only take what we can carry. It's a two-day walk under the Black Mountain to the Third State.'

In five minutes, we were ready to go. Jack picked up his nerf gun.

'Locked and loaded, Ma,' he said.

'Good, Jack-boy. Here kids, you take these.' Mrs P gave Nala and me smaller, modified nerf guns and a big belt bag of biscuit bullets, which we tied onto our waists.

'Brilliant! Thanks.' I took mine and pumped the primer.

'Awesome!' Nala grinned.

'Time to say goodbye to this old place,' Mrs P said, and picked up her own nerf-machine gun. 'It's such a shame to leave all our things for the gangsters to steal. No, I can't do it!' She pumped up her gun and took aim.

Bam-bam-bam-bam-bam-bam-bam-bam-bam-bam.

We watched as she tore up her old sitting room with bullets. All around us plates and cups broke apart, glasses and windows shattered and, *total tragedy*, the flat screen TV exploded.

'Hey, Ma. No!' Jack wailed.

'We can't take it, Jack boy, and we're never coming back.'

Bam-bam-bam-bam-bam-bam-bam-bam-bam-bam.

She finished the job off.

'Now, time to roll out!' commanded Mrs P, and she pulled on her aviator shades. 'Advance on foot to the ute.'

I didn't remember ever having had a mum, but I wished she had been as cool as Mrs P.

11

GANGSTER NUMERO UNO

Half an hour later, I was sitting in the open back of the truck. Mrs P was driving (only we weren't moving) and Jack was sitting shotgun. We couldn't get close to Brick Alley because there was a traffic jam of people, cars, trolleys, and bikes blocking the narrow road. There must have been a thousand families.

'Fat crap! See what you've done, you idiot,' Jack said through the open back window. 'Now every loser in the Shambles has beaten us to it.'

'No point in blaming Zanto now, Jack,' Mrs P said. 'We are where we are. If only we knew what was happening at the front.'

'I'll go and check it out,' I said and jumped out.

'I'll come too,' Nala said.

She pulled on her NFL helmet and I put my visor down. She held her pool cue, I had my baseball bat, and we had our guns slung over our shoulders.

We walked down the long crush of people—mums and dads, old folks, their vehicles, their children, their animals, and their belongings. One truck was piled so high with furniture, chairs, tables and mattresses, all held on with ropes, that it looked like it would tip over. An old man was sitting on a motorbike with his wife, and a grumpy-looking, pot-bellied pig was squeezed into the side-car. Another family was wheeling all it could in shopping trolleys. They didn't know that they couldn't take it into the tunnel with them. Mrs P said that the only way in was down a steep spiral staircase with two hundred steps.

Everyone looked scared, talking in quiet voices, wondering how they would find the tunnel, knowing they had to get past GN1, and that the zombies might attack at any moment. They knew their old life was over forever, that the Shambles might not even exist tomorrow. I saw all kinds of different emotions—sadness, anger, fear, bravery—people leaving everything behind and heading into the scary unknown because they had to. Knowing they'd have to find a new life somehow, somewhere, in some place they'd never even visited before. And they had to hope the people there were kind to them. I felt as scared as them. What kind of life would it be?

Nala and I zigzagged our way through the crowd, getting closer to the entrance of Brick Alley.

'What the problem?' I asked a man.

'There's a block across the road. The gangster isn't letting anyone into Brick Alley,' he said.

An argument broke out between two families, jostling for position in the queue. The dads were talking loud, sweating in the heat, and pushing each other. One mum was trying to stop it, but the other was pushing too. They were screaming and swearing at each other, and some of the kids were crying, frightened. There was no way my Dad would act like those grown-ups.

'Zanto, get ready quick!' Nala pointed. She was already in warrior pose.

Five zombies, three men and two women, were staggering down a side street towards the noise, but the grown-ups nearby were too busy fighting each other to notice. Kids behind us started to scream. The zombies ran at us. It was too late to reach for our nerf guns.

Hiyah!

Nala stuck her cue in the ground, twirled on it, and

roundhouse-kicked the head of the first lady zombie. The dead woman hit the dust groaning—she wasn't getting up again any time soon.

Kerchow!

I did a perfect fullback's tackle, taking out the legs of the nearest slobbering guy, and he fell to the floor. Two of the kids nearby jumped onto him and pulled him away. Nala wiped out a girl zombie with a twirl of her stick. Some huge fat jelly zombie was waddling towards her, his yellow fangs dripping. I took out my catapult and fired a stone at his backside. He yelped, tried to look at his backside and fell to the floor.

Nala somersaulted, and landed on his back, knocking the air out of him at both ends. He gave out a massive fart and burp and collapsed like a deflated balloon—out for the count. The stench was beyond bad. Nala got a round of applause from the crowd, and she bowed, still standing on the zombie's back and holding her nose.

We'd done it! I counted the unconscious zombies—one, two three, four… Hang-on, weren't there five of them?

'Grr- whhaaa-yaaah!'

I was bowled over onto my back by the hideous creature. All the air was knocked out of me. Next, the lurching foul-smelling zombie was dragging me back down the alley. I tried kicking it, but no good. Then my head was inside its putrid, sweating hairy armpit.

'Get off me!' I yelled.

'Grr-whhaaa-yaaah.'

I was turned upside down, then back upright again. I was dizzy, and I couldn't reach my nerf gun. My neck was in the zombie's massive hand. I saw a skull and cross bones tattooed on the huge arm. I couldn't breathe; my vision blurred as its nose touched mine. I tried to focus on its big angry green face. I saw the tattoo on his head—"S-MAN". Crap! S-Man was going to eat my head. He opened his mouth wide, and his breath was almost enough to knock me out.

'S-Man, it's me *Zero*, Romeo's kid brother. I fetched you pizzas. Don't eat me!'

And then he…then he…then he…*didn't* eat me. Instead, he seemed to be searching me for something, his mad red eyes frantic.

'Is this what you want?' I held up the scull catapult.

S-Man's red eyes lit up looking almost for a moment like he was alive. His hands, with their lethal talons, snatched at the catapult. Nala was right, he really did love it. And who could blame him? It was ultra-cool. Nala raced up, her nerf gun ready.

'No, it's alright; he's an okay one, despite being a psycho when he was alive,' I said. 'Here you go then, good S-Man.' I held the catapult up and he watched it like he was being hypnotised. 'Fetch!'

I threw it back down the alley, away from the people.

S-Man chased after then picked up his catapult and sat down on the dirt road, stroking it. Nala was still keeping guard with her biscuit gun, and behind us the crowd was watching, fascinated. I stood up. Now he had what he wanted, S-Man was happy to sit quiet. I could swear he was smiling—only some sort of berserk, yellow-fanged, and slobbery smile.

'Nice one, kids,' someone yelled, and there was some clapping.

Suddenly, there was a commotion in the road. It was as if a Mexican wave rippled through the crowd. Only rather than people standing and waving their arms up, they were making space to let someone through and closing again afterward. Whoever was coming, people wanted to get away from him fast. The crowd parted right in front of us, and he arrived—Gangster Numero Uno.

GN1 was tall and thin, with short white-blonde hair and pale skin, like he'd never been in the sun. He was dressed in a white shirt and black suit. I'd only seen him from a distance before, and I wished it had stayed that way, because up close, he was too scary. He didn't pull faces, or nothing, but there was something about him that you knew was dangerous. His eyes seemed too blue, and he stared like he could get inside your head and steal your thoughts.

First, GN1 looked at the wiped-out zombies, then at Nala and me, and last at S-Man. There was no expression on his face. One of the knocked-out zombies began to wake up. GN1 bent down and picked up a rock.

Thunk.

Without looking, he threw the rock at the zombie's head. It fell back onto the dirt, unconscious again. GN1 turned back to the crowd and spoke to them.

'Seems as we have lots of squatters on my patch, don't it?' His voice was loud, so everyone could hear. 'Guess you all want to escape *the bomb*? You all want to get out through the tunnel?'

'Yes!' came cries from all around.

Gangster Numero Uno laughed, and it was the most horrible sound I've ever heard—worse than the zombies snarling. It took all the hope out of your heart.

'Do you know where the entrance is?' a lady called out.

'Course I know! I've been using it for years to bring in my goods,' GN1 laughed again.

I knew what *goods* he meant. It was *bads* more like— drink, drugs, and guns—all the stuff he sold to Romeo and the other kids. Everything that had made my brother forget his studies, forget that he was supposed to get a good job and look after his dad.

'Will you help us escape?' someone asked.

'Sure, I will, if you got the dollars. Because it's *my*

tunnel!' GN1 roared. 'And no one gets through, unless you pay the fee.'

'How much?' someone called.

'Two thousand dollars for each living body, whether a baby, granny, animal, or whatever. I don't care who or what. No discounts. No negotiations.'

There was a murmur from the crowd. Perhaps two thousand dollars wasn't much for someone who worked in the Iron City, but for people in the Shambles it was huge, as much as my dad earned in a year.

'What if we don't have enough money?' the old man with the pot-bellied pig asked. GN1 laughed again.

'**Boom!**' he cried, and made an explosion with his hands.

'You can't leave people trapped here,' Nala said.

'Watch me,' GN1 snorted.

'But they'll die…' Nala said and stepped towards him. I pulled on her sleeve to keep her back.

'Tell someone what cares, little girl.'

Nala looked at him in disbelief. I guess she'd never known that such evil people existed for real.

'You'll never get away with doing something so wicked,' Nala said. 'You'll get punished.'

GN1 stepped towards her. I was scared for Nala then because she didn't know just what this man could do.

'Who by? You and your wimpy boyfriend?'

Whoa, wait. *Wimpy? Boyfriend?* No way!

'No, you'll be punished by someone *more powerful* than you!'

'Like who?'

'Like the Law, or Il Presido, or God!' Nala cried.

'Really?' GN1 leaned down to her and whispered so that only we could hear. 'I don't see none of them around here sweetheart. Perhaps God, or Allah, or Buddha is coming to save you, but I don't think so. And Il Presido sure isn't stepping foot in the Shambles. He'll stay safe in his palace. In the real world, there are no heroes, and no one cares about you kids or these other fools.'

'My dad cares!' I shouted.

GN1 looked around. 'And where is he?'

'Well then, *I* care!' I said.

'I'm not too worried about what you might do, son.' GN1 shrugged. 'I'm the only hope these people have, but I'm a businessman. If they pay, they'll escape; if not, they won't.'

'You better watch out because bad guys never win in the end!' Nala said.

'Wise-up, sweetheart,' GN1 laughed again. 'The bad guys always win around here. I'm not going down—not in this story.'

He walked away again through the Mexican wave.

'Pay up or stay here and die!' he called behind him.

All around us, people started to panic. Some shot forward, pushing to the front.

'We have the money,' they cried.

Others were scrambling through packed belongings, pulling whatever they could carry off their cars, and collecting jewellery or valuables they could possibly pay with. But the worst thing was seeing those who sat on the dusty ground, staring into space—the folk who had no money and nothing valuable to offer instead. There was no escape for them. It wasn't right, and it wasn't fair. I wished I could help them, but I couldn't.

12

DESPERATE MEASURES

Back in Mrs P's truck, we counted out how much money we had. We needed eight thousand dollars. Between us, we had six thousand in cash and the watches and jewellery Nala had brought, which she said were worth almost three thousand. It was just enough.

'But that means we'll have nothing left to start our new life,' I said.

'I told you to bring all the stuff from the shop,' Jack said, grumpily.

'Here he is,' Mrs P said.

One of GN1's gangsters came up to us. We handed over all our money and he gave us a yellow ticket each.

'Aren't you ashamed?' Nala asked him. But he never bothered to reply.

'Okay, kids, we've got our tickets. Let's roll,' Mrs P said. 'If we get separated, make for the Capital City. Go to '*Ye Olde Candy Shoppe*' in the East Quarter—I have friends there who'll help us.'

'Okay, Ma,' Jack said.

We were loaded up with bags and packs on our fronts and backs. We carried our weapons too and had extra bags of biscuit bullets. We set off, leaving the truck behind, the doors wide open. We'd left our homes, and now we had to leave behind everything we couldn't carry, too.

People with no money were just sitting on the side of the road. Jack was right; not everyone was going to survive, but only because GN1 cared about money and nothing else. He could've let them all escape the bomb. Instead, his men took their yellow tickets at the gate and only let in those who had money. About fifty meters up the alley, people were being moved into an old garage.

'That's the entrance to the tunnel,' Mrs P said.

A fight broke out. People trying to get in who had no money. No chance. The gangsters had no mercy. They shoved and threw them backwards. It was awful.

Suddenly, a terrible noise wailed through the air! Have you ever heard an air raid warning? I hope not. It's the most terrifying noise I've ever heard—a long low sound that grows really loud and then shrinks again, like a moving wave.

'The bomb's coming!' someone shouted. 'The zombies must be breaking down the South Gate.'

Panic spread through those already in Brick Alley and those of us waiting to get in. The people who couldn't pay started to run towards the queue too. Everyone was screaming loud and pushing. We were being crushed. I squeezed out to the side, and Nala followed me, but we lost Jack and Mrs P.

We watched as people fought and pushed to get into the alley. And that's when GN1's men lost control. The barrier fell over, the crowd pushed past, and the gangsters ran away into the tunnel. I was relieved that those with no money could escape too, but worried people would be hurt in the stampede. Then we heard the screams from the back of the crowd! There were about fifty zombies coming up from behind.

'Nala, quick!' I yelled at her and we dropped our bags.

We ran and took up our positions as the slavering green creatures staggered up to us.

Pah-pah-pah-pow.

Nala started taking the zombies out with her super nerf gun. Four of them crashed down, knocked unconscious. She was a great shot.

Zap-Zap.

I shot twice and missed twice. A lurching green woman ran towards me. Her black talons were dripping with blood. She was a man-eater for sure. I aimed.

Zap.

I missed again. She was nearly at me.

Pah-pah-pow-pah-pow.

'Come on Zanto,' Nala cried as she took down five more zombies. 'Imagine it's the goal and you have to score.'

I saw the goal on the woman's head.

Zap.

A biscuit bullet hit her right between the eyes, and she zonked back asleep onto the dirt.

'He shoots, he scores!' I yelled.

'Nice one, Reygo,' Nala laughed.

Pah-pah-pow-pah-pow.

Zap. Zap. Zap. Zap. Zap.

We took down ten more zombies before they could reach the crowd. Then in the distance, high above, we saw a huge air force plane approaching and heard the low roar of its engines. Behind us, the crowd was thinning as everyone raced down into the tunnel. Another hundred or so zombies appeared behind us. We couldn't fight them all.

'Zanto, quick, we have to go,' Nala called.

We picked up our bags and ran towards Brick Alley, with the zombie hoard chasing after. The last few people were going into the garage. They were closing the doors behind them to keep the charging zombies out. They hadn't seen us.

'No wait!' we yelled. Then we saw Jack.

'Stop!' he ordered. 'Wait for my friends!'

The zombies were racing after us, as fast as their stumbling legs would allow. We reached the doors and just managed to get inside. Jack slammed them shut after us.

'Thanks, G-Nut,' I cried.

'Yeah, thanks,' Nala said.

Everyone else was already running down the spiral stairs.

'As if I'd go without you,' he said. 'But where's Ma?'

'Isn't she with you?' Nala said.

'I thought she went to help *you*,' he said. 'We've got to go back out and look for her.'

But the zombies outside started screaming and banging on the wooden doors. The doors began to creak and bend—they wouldn't last long.

'I'm sorry mate,' I said to him, 'but we have to go. We'll die if we stay here.' Jack looked devastated. 'Perhaps Mrs P's already in the tunnel looking for you.'

'Your Ma said, if we lost each other, to meet at Ye Olde Candy Shoppe,' Nala reminded him. The wooden door began to split open. A zombie claw came through, its black talons reaching for us.

'We have to go, Jack,' Nala took G-Nut's hand. 'Your

Ma would want you to escape.'

The door burst open and the zombie hoard fell in, chasing our flesh.

While the zombies fell in a pile at the doorway, we clattered down the spiral staircase into the darkness. There were about two hundred steps. When we reached the bottom, we were in the tunnel. At the opening were two huge open iron gates. We were the last ones. Once inside, we closed the gates behind us and locked them. Even if the zombies could work out how to get their uncontrollable legs down the staircase, they couldn't follow. We could breathe easy for a while, but it was too dark to see anything. I took out my torch and shone it ahead of us. It reminded me of Dad again and of how he always believed in me. I hoped he was safe in the Third State, at the end of the tunnel. That gave me the strength to keep going.

The tunnel was wide enough for four people, and it seemed to run straight for as long as I could see. Now we were underground and on our journey, everyone seemed calmer. There had been many hundreds of families trying to get out of the Shambles, and I thought that most had made it. Now, they were all walking quietly into the darkness ahead. It was hard to believe that two days ago everyone had been safe in their homes, eating dinner or watching TV. No one had imagined they'd have to leave everything behind and hope for the kindness of strangers at the end of their journey.

'Ma, Ma, it's Jack. Are you there?' G-Nut called. His cry echoed off the walls, but there was no reply.

'Come on, mate, it's a massive crowd. If she's near the front, she'll never hear you,' I put my arm around Jack's shoulder. 'She'll be waiting for you at the Candy Shoppe. We'll find her on the other side.'

Jack shrugged me off and walked on ahead. I knew to leave him alone.

BOOM!

There was a huge explosion above us; the ground shook like an earthquake, and dust rained down onto us. A few people cried out, but most stayed quiet, stunned and frightened. The bomb had been dropped! The Shambles was gone, and so were all those poor Infected whether they were man-eaters or not.

I hoped Mrs P was safe somewhere in the tunnel. I thought of the zombie mum trying to feed me with her wooden spoon, and S-Man with his catapult, and Romeo, probably still hating me. I thought of how proud Dad had been of the home he'd made for us. It may have been tiny and poor, but we'd been happy there. I thought of my friends on the MSC soccer team. We'd played together every Saturday, and dreamed of playing for

Real Magique, or Pooltown, or Barcelino, or Manfield United, or Marsonne. Were they even alive now? Our whole world had gone forever.

'Come on, Zanto,' Nala took my hand. 'We've escaped, we're alive, and we've still got our dreams. No one can take those away from us.'

We joined the others and walked on into the unknown.

13

ESCAPE

We didn't find Mrs P on that long walk through the tunnel. Jack didn't speak much, though we tried to comfort him. We mostly walked in the dark to save the torch battery. I guess I knew something was wrong with me before we reached the end of the journey. I wasn't hungry, when I was usually starving, and I started to feel dizzy and hot. It was getting harder to breathe too, but I supposed that was because it was stuffy in the tunnel. I needed to rest more than the others, when I used to be able to run for two hours without caring. I just didn't feel right. Of course, I didn't realise then what was actually happening to me.

Towards the end of the second day, the dark started to seem a bit brighter. Then we heard excited voices ahead of us.

'It's the end of the tunnel,' Nala said. 'We've made it. Come on.'

She ran ahead in excitement. Jack chased after her, hoping to find his Ma at last. I tried to run too, but fell onto my face. It was as if my legs didn't work properly. I stood up and limped slowly after them. I was the last one out of the tunnel.

I reached the exit and looked out, but closed my eyes again tight. It was grey outside and pouring with rain, but even that amount of light burnt my eyes. It made me want to roar with anger. I dropped my bag, my boots fell to the floor, and my football rolled away. I didn't care. I screwed up my eyes and managed to focus.

We were in an enclosure, completely fenced off. The army was there. They had tents set up, one with a huge red cross on it. Everyone who came out of the tunnel was queuing to go into a medical tent. As they waited, they were given a bottle of water, a sandwich, and a clear plastic poncho with a hood to keep the rain off. As I watched, some people were led out of the medical tent to the right side and taken onto a bus. They seemed… not *happy*—none of us could be happy—but relieved that someone was looking after them.

There were people outside the fence too, locals of the Third State I guessed. Most of them had brought blankets, coats, and food, and were giving it out to the folk getting on the bus. They had signs, like *'Welcome to the Third State'* and *'You're safe now'*. But, there were others holding up signs that weren't kind, but cruel and insulting, like *'Not welcome'*, *'Go home'*, and *'No Infected scum here'*. They were shouting at us, too, and waving their fists.

I'd never thought that people in Third State wouldn't want to help us. Where else could we go? I was certain that, if the Third State had been infected, we folk from the Shambles would have helped those people. Wouldn't we?

I stopped in shock because I saw Gangster Numero Uno sitting on the bus, looking like a regular guy escaping the bomb. He stared back, daring me to give him up. I tried to run to the soldiers, to tell them that he was a gangster, a criminal, and should be sent to jail. Only my legs wouldn't work. I slammed down into the mud. When I managed to stand up, his bus had gone, and a new empty one had arrived. GN1 had escaped!

I tried to catch up with Jack and Nala.

'Ma's not here,' G-Nut said. 'I know she wouldn't leave without me. She must have been killed by the bomb!'

I felt so bad for him. He looked like he'd been crying.

'Don't give up hope yet, Jack, she still might be okay,' Nala said. 'They're not letting anyone stay and wait. If she made it through, she'll head to the Candy Shoppe.' She looked at me. 'Zanto are you okay? You look a strange colour, and your eyes are all red.'

'Just tired,' I said. My voice sounded more like a growl.

We joined the back of the queue. News was being passed down the line.

'*The zombies broke out of the Shambles before the bomb fell—most of them got away. The Iron City is overrun now, but they're building a new wall around it. They haven't had any outbreaks here in the Third State yet, but they're not taking any risks. They won't let us in unless we test as uninfected.*'

A family came out of the medical tent. I remember them because they were all so blonde—a mum, dad, and three teenagers. They weren't sent to the bus. Instead, they were taken to the left, to another tent, and they weren't happy at all about it. The kids were crying and the dad was angry, struggling and shouting. They didn't want to go, but I couldn't hear what they were saying.

'Infected!' Someone said.

'What's going to happen to them?' Nala wondered.

No one knew.

I had the worst headache ever, with shooting pains behind my eyes. I needed to lie down and sleep. At last, we made it to the front of the queue and went inside the medical tent. We watched a mum and baby ahead of us.

The nurse put a cotton bud in the baby's mouth. Then he wiped it on a glass plate and gave it to another man with a microscope. A lady doctor took its temperature and looked into its eyes with a bright light. The baby cried.

'All clear,' the man with the microscope said.

'All clear here,' the doctor said.

The mum was okay too, but she cried anyway. A soldier took them through the exit on the right for the bus.

'What happens to them now?' Nala asked.

'They go to the refugee camp, along with everyone else who escaped the Second State,' the nurse said. 'There are thousands of people needing a new home.'

'You next,' the doctor pointed at me.

I sat down, and the nurse put the cotton bud in my mouth.

'His teeth are sharp,' he said.

The doctor took my temperature.

'Way too high,' she said and shone the light in my eyes.

It burned me. I roared and screamed at her. She jumped back. Nala and Jack looked at me like strangely.

'Zero, stay cool man,' G-Nut said.

'He's turning green,' the doctor said. 'And his eyes are red. What does his test say?'

'Infected!' The microscope man said.

What? How? I felt like someone had zapped me with an electric shock. The two soldiers pointed their guns at me.

'Don't move,' they shouted.

'But he hasn't been bitten,' Nala cried. 'He can't be infected!'

'You don't need to be bitten, just body fluid contact,' the doctor said. 'Have you had infected spit or vomit on you?'

Through my fog, I remembered Romeo and his vile snot.

'One sneezed on me,' I said. 'Am I going to die? Am I going to be one of them?'

I looked at my fingernails and I knew the answer already—they were long and black. I looked at my skin—I *was* green. Then I was very scared.

'I'm sorry, there's no cure,' the doctor said.

I slumped onto my backside on the floor. The doctor turned to Nala and Jack.

'Have you two had any contact with him, held hands, shared food?'

'No!' Jack stepped back, his eyes darting all around the room, looking for a way to escape. 'We haven't, have we?' He looked at Nala.

'Yes,' she sounded as scared as I felt. 'We shared ice-creams remember—spit.'

'Fat crap!' Jack swore and made a run for the tent exit. A big soldier grabbed him and brought him back. The nurse put a cotton bud in Nala's mouth.

'Infected too!' The Microscope man said.

'But I wanted to be a doctor...' She sat down next to me.

'I'm so sorry,' I said to her. It was my fault. I'd made her lick the ice cream.

Jack was kicking and struggling, but he couldn't escape. 'Infected!'

'It's all your fault, Zero!' Jack yelled at me. 'You've made us all zombies.'

'It's not his fault, Lamebrain,' Nala said. 'You were the one who wanted ice cream. I told you not to.'

My head hurt too much to shout and argue.

'What are you going to do to us now?' Nala asked.

'Shoot us, that's what!' Jack yelled.

'Don't be silly. We don't harm children,' the doctor said. 'They'll take you to a safe place where you'll be looked after.'

The soldier pulled us up.

'Time to go kids, and don't even think about running.'

We were led in the opposite direction to the mum and baby. Just when we thought we'd escaped to a new life, we were doomed.

Nala took my hand, and we walked out of the left door. The soldiers took us to the other tent and opened the flap. Inside, there was a huge cage full of kids who looked just as scared as us, but no adults. The soldiers opened the cage door, put us inside, and then locked it again behind us. We were in prison.

Jack held onto the bars and yelled and kicked, but they just ignored him. I was so tired I sat down on the floor. Nala held my hand.

'You'll be okay, Zanto,' she whispered.

But we both knew she was wrong.

'Where are all the infected grown-ups?' Nala asked a lad next to us. It was the blonde boy we'd seen before.

'Don't know. They took our mum and dad away in a truck,' he said. 'What does any of it matter now? We're all dead anyway.' He stared into space.

He was right. We were all going to be zombies soon. I wished I'd been able to say goodbye to Dad, wished I'd seen Reygo play. But then I felt so ill that I didn't care about anything much. I just wanted to sleep.

'I need to lie down for a bit,' I said.

And so, I did, on the floor; anything to stop my head pounding.

I think I remember being in the back of a truck, feeling it rock and hearing the noisy engine as we bounced along. Then it seemed like we were on a boat. I could hear gulls, and waves. We were rising and falling so that my stomach could feel it. Then I was unconscious.

* * * *

I was lying on a bed staring at tent canvas. I was hot and cold, shaking and sweating. It was night, and Nala was sitting next to me. There was a light on, so they had electricity here.

'Zanto? You've been asleep for hours,' she said. 'We've been sent to *the Island*. We're in a camp for infected orphans. The kids here in the hospital are waiting to turn into zombies. And when they do, they put you in there... *the Pen*.'

She sounded scared. I looked where she was pointing. Through the window, I could see tall strong fences covered with barbed wire. Behind them, were green, red-eyed zombie kids all standing around snarling, and roaring at the lights. There was a tall tower with a guard and gun watching them. It was a prison.

'Zanto, are you feeling better? Can't you speak?' She held my hand.

I tried to talk, but I didn't have the energy. I just

wanted to sleep. She put her hand on my head.

'You're too hot. I'll get the nurse,' her voice was fading.
I was so tired.

'Zanto?' Nala's voice was fading away, and the blood was rushing through my head. 'Someone help him! Zanto, don't die! Remember your dreams, you're going to play for Real Magique. You're going to meet Reygo and find your dad again. Oh no. Somebody quick. He needs CPR!'

And then, at last, her voice went quiet and my head stopped hurting.

I guess that was when I died.

14

DEAD

I don't know how long I was dead for, but after a while I woke up again—only not fully. My memories of that time are fuzzy. Of course, I didn't realise I was a zombie. It seemed like I was in a dream and was seeing the world through misty dark red glasses, because everything seemed like fuzzy night-vision—nothing was in focus. And I couldn't understand anything I heard.

I was lying on my back staring at the sky, and it was raining. I guess I must have been dumped into the Pen. I yelled at the daylight, as I didn't like it—it hurt my eyes. I stood up slowly, as my legs hardly knew how to work. I walked unsteadily through the mud until I came to a fence. I rattled it, but couldn't get through, and I didn't know how to turn around, so I just stayed there, bashing my head against the wire.

The next day, someone walked into me and I bounced off the wire. Now I was facing the other way. And so, I walked in *that* direction, until I came to a wooden building that I couldn't get past, and I bounced off that. Thinking about it now, I must have been like a big and slow steel ball in a giant pinball machine. It keeps going until it hits something and then crashes off in another direction. I don't know how long I did that for, but weeks I think.

I was in the middle of a crowd of zombie kids, all bouncing off each other, growling, and screaming. Looking back now, I realise that we weren't making those noises because we were angry or aggressive, just because that was our language then. Because living humans didn't understand it, they assumed that we were furious and blood thirsty.

There was a loud noise above us. We looked up, and there was a huge noisy thing, which made a wind that sounded like *whop-whop-whop* and pushed us over (I guess now it was a helicopter). It dropped pieces of meat down on us, and everyone near me scrambled to grab some and eat it. But I didn't like meat when I was alive, and I didn't like it now. So instead, I ate the grass.

At night, there were tall bright lights that hurt my eyes. I wanted them to be turned off, so I screamed and yelled at them. There were other kids all around too, screeching at the lights. They were green with yellow fangs and red eyes. Somehow, I knew they were zombies, only I wasn't scared of them anymore. I bawled at them to say hello, and they did it back. Then it was morning again, and I carried on walking.

Weeks later, I banged into the fence again. There were some kids on the other side, not green, but alive. A couple of the zombies went berserk when they saw them, tried to pull the fence down, because they wanted to eat them. But others, like me, just yelled to say hello. I remember seeing a boy with a football. The only thought in my head was that I wanted that ball, and I wanted to play soccer. I hissed and shook the fence.

'*Let me play too*,' I tried to say. But as I could only growl and roar, the kids were scared and ran off. I can imagine now what they saw. A green zombie with mad red eyes and gnashing fangs, snarling at them and trying to get through the fence to *attack* them. Only I never wanted to hurt them, I just wanted the ball. It was all I could think of. I guess I was like S-Man and his catapult.

I turned and walked in the other direction, until I hit another fence. Then a siren went off, and I had to walk towards the loud noise and scream at it, because I thought it was trying to talk to me.

I only had enough brainpower for one thought, and my one thing was always—*find a football*. Sometimes I bashed into a skinny green zombie girl with long black braids, and it was like I knew her, or wanted to know her, but all we could do was snarl at each other. Then we would bounce off and keep walking again, until we had to turn around. I walked every day, with only that one thought...

'*Find a football. Find a football. Find a football. Find a football.*'

One day, it was hot and the sun was hurting my eyes, so I roared at it. I reached the fence and, outside, I saw the normal kids playing soccer again. I was pressed against the wire, calling at them to let me play. The other zombies were screeching at them too. The kids were kicking the ball at the fence, probably teasing us. The ball flew too high and over the fence. It bounced off the hard dirt, and rolled away. All the other zombies ignored it. The kids ran away.

'*Find a football. Find a football. Find a football. Find a football.*'

I staggered towards the ball and picked it up. At last, I had a football. And that was when my one thought changed to...

'*Keepy-uppy. Keepy-uppy. Keepy-uppy. Keepy-uppy. Keepy-uppy.*'

At first, I was rubbish. My legs would hardly work, and I kept dropping the ball. I would snarl and scream at it, then pick it up again. But each day, my legs started to remember a bit more how to move. Soon, I could keep the ball up, first off my feet, then knees, and then onto my shoulder and head. Sometimes the zombie chick with black braids would stop screaming and watch me. Then, one day, my only thought changed…

'*Dribble. Dribble. Dribble. Dribble. Dribble. Dribble. Dribble.*'

By then, my legs were working fast. Instead of walking up to the fence and bouncing off in another direction, now I would run a bit, with the ball at my feet, dribbling. I could zigzag the football around the other staggering zombies. The more I ran, the stronger I felt. But still my world was hazy. And then, my thought changed again…

'*Score. Score. Score. Score. Score. Score. Score. Score. Score.*'

There was a place on the fence that looked like two goal posts. All day and night, I kicked the football at the goal, and scored over, and over, and over, because that's all I ever thought of. I tried to pass the ball to the zombie with black braids, but she only stood still and snarled at me, her yellow fangs dripping.

One day, I was scoring goals, when a gate in the fence opened and a huge truck roared in. The hungry angry zombies raced towards it screaming, but they were pushed back by a giant blast of water from a canon that knocked them over. Big men jumped out of the truck. A lady with a white coat pointed, and they walked towards me. I held my football and snarled at them. There was a loud shot and something hurt me. I looked down and roared. There was a dart sticking out of my leg. Now I was scared. I raced towards them snarling, trying to tell them to leave me alone, but then the next minute, I was flat on my face in the mud. Snoring.

When I awoke, I was lying on a hard surface. There were bright lights hurting my eyes, and I could see fuzzy shapes and shadows moving around me. I tried to move, but I couldn't. There was something holding me down. I growled and spat. I could hear sounds—I guess people talking—but I couldn't understand. There was a sharp prick in my arm. I struggled and snarled. And then a terrible pain shot through my heart that made me scream. I shuddered and shook, as if I was full of electricity. Everything went black again.

15

AWOKEN

I opened my eyes. I was on a soft mattress, and I could hear a low gentle sound that made me feel happy. I remembered that sound from another life. It was *music!* I opened my eyes, and the burning pain had gone. It was daylight, and it didn't hurt. I still couldn't focus that well, but the fuzzy red mist had gone. I sat up, looked around, and gradually, my eyes began to focus. I could see like normal again.

I was in a hospital room, with a table and chair and lots of strange-looking machines. There was a tube in my arm connected to a bag on a trolley. A wire was sticky-taped to my green finger and connected to a black computer monitor. There was a green line moving across the screen that kept jumping up in a squiggle and double bleeping. It sounded like a heartbeat. I kicked off the bed sheets and looked at my legs. They were green and covered in black scabs. In fact, my whole body was covered in scabs.

I climbed out of the bed. My legs were wobbly, but they worked. I pulled the trolley with me and walked over to a mirror.

Argg!

I jumped when I saw myself. My face was green and covered in scabs, my eyes red, and my teeth sharp and yellow. I was a zombie for sure.

'*But am I dead?*' I wondered.

There was a band around my wrist with '*Z51*' written on it. I pulled the wire off my finger. The green line on the monitor went flat and gave a long loud warning alarm. I could hear people running in the corridor outside. I stepped back into the corner, nervous of what might happen next. The door opened and two nurses and a doctor ran in. They all stopped when they saw me.

We stared at each other for what seemed like ages, and then the doctor smiled at me and switched off the alarm.

'Hello Z51,' she said. 'How do you feel today?'

I tried to speak, but didn't know how to make any words.

'If you understand me, raise your hand,' she said.

I could do that. The doctor laughed and one of the nurses clapped.

'I'm Doctor Allen. Are you hungry?' she asked.

I nodded. I was starving. Dr Allen took a banana from a bowl and held it out for me. I leaned forward until I could reach it, and then snatched it from her. I wolfed it down.

'What's your name?' The doctor asked me.

I frowned and tried to remember. But I couldn't.

'Doooon't knooooow,' I said. The words were slurred but I understood them. I couldn't remember when I'd last made a sound that wasn't a snarl.

Dr Allen smiled again.

'You can speak now. That's new. I told you your name yesterday—it's Z51.'

I couldn't remember yesterday.

'Zeeedddd,' was all I could manage.

'You're a very lucky boy, Z51.'

'Whhhhy?'

'Because you're not dead anymore. We awoke you two weeks ago.'

'I'mmm aaaliiive?' I asked and put my hand to my heart. I could feel it beating.

'Yes.'

'How looooong was I deeeead?' The words were getting easier now.

'Six months,' Dr Allen said. 'You were in a bad way, lots of rotting flesh. But when the scabs fall off, you'll be whole again.'

'But stiiiill greeeen?'

'Probably, but here's a picture we took before you first awoke, see how your skin has regenerated since then.'

The doctor held out the photo. I walked towards her slowly and took it.

It made me shudder. My mouth was wide open like I was screaming, with dark yellow sharp fangs, and my eyes red and raving. My skin was bright green and covered with yellow boils, with rotting bits of flesh hanging off. My nails were an inch long, black, and twisted.

I looked in the mirror, and at least I didn't look as bad now. I was green, but not such a strong shade, and I had no boils. The whites of my eyes were still a bit red, but the iris was brown again. My teeth were sharp and still a bit long, but not really fangs anymore, and they were a paler yellow. My nails were black, but cut short.

'Sooo, am I cuuured?'

'Not really,' Doctor Allen said. 'You still have the zombie mutation in your blood, but your heart is beating again, and you don't seem dangerous. I'd call you an *Awoken*.'

'Hooow did you wake me uuup?' My words came out faster as I was remembering.

'We identified an anti-virus drug that could fight the infection. However, to our surprise, when we injected you, it restarted your heart like we'd jolted you with electricity. You've made history, Z51. Though you aren't 100% human, you are alive again. And you're not infectious anymore—no danger to others. You give us hope that one day we might find a total cure. Now get some rest.'

Doctor Allen came back the next day. By then, I could speak easily, like my brain had warmed up. She gave me some tests, like asking me to read an ABC learner and do some sums. I could do the easiest sums, like 1 plus 1, but I couldn't read the book. I'd forgotten all my letters. I felt stupid.

'My brother always said I was dumb,' I said.

'Never mind, perhaps you'll remember later,' Dr Allen smiled.

'Are we still on the Island?' I asked her.

'Yes.'

'In the zombie prison for kids?'

'It's a hospital, not a prison,' she said.

'But there's barbed wire, and we're not allowed out,' I said. 'So, it's really a prison. What happened to all the infected grownups they rounded up?'

Dr Allen looked cautious.

'They were sent to the Iron City, and a wall was built to keep them in,' she said after a bit. 'They were going to turn into zombies anyway.'

'Was I the first kid you experimented on?' I asked.

'No. We tried the medicine on others, but it didn't

work. I decided that we needed to pick a child who showed some signs of higher brain function. You were able to control a football, when all the others could only stagger around. So, we picked you.'

I laughed. Never in my life before had anyone said I had a higher brain function.

'I'm just good at football,' I told her, 'even when I'm dead.'

The doctor did some more tests. Then she sat down again.

'So, what was it like being dead, Z51? Did you want to kill humans?'

'No, mostly I just wanted to play football, or I was confused and scared.'

'So why do the other zombies kill?' she asked me.

'I don't know,' I said. 'But not all zombies turn bad.' I told her about the mum zombie.

'She just wanted to feed me. She was a nice dead person, and I think most of the other zombies are like me and her. They don't chase living humans because they want to kill them, but perhaps they just want to be part of… the *gang*. Only they just didn't know how.

'When you're screaming and growling, you think you're talking; only it scares living people. And the zombies keep running towards you, because they don't know what else to do. They certainly don't all attack you. But I guess when you're alive, you're too scared to wait and find that out.

'They dropped a bomb on the Shambles to kill all the Infected, but I hope the harmless ones got away.'

'Yes, I know about the bomb,' the doctor said, 'but it didn't work. They won't drop anymore.'

'Why?'

'It only destroyed the zombies directly underneath. And the heat of the explosion caused a new mutation in all the Infected it missed. They became even stronger, like *super-zombies*, and *definitely* man-eaters. There was a cannibal zombie hoard almost out of control, but the army managed to build the wall around the Iron City in time to keep them contained. The city is a huge prison now. There's no way to kill the new mutated zombies with normal weapons anymore. That's why we turned to researching the disease. We began experimenting to try and, and, and—*cure* the Infection. You're our first breakthrough.'

'So, what will happen to me now?' I asked. 'Can I leave the Island and go and look for my dad. He might still be in the Third State.'

'I don't know. I'll need to ask Capo Grey,' she said.

'Who's Capo Grey?' I asked.

'He governs this camp. But for now, get some rest, Z51.'

'Zanto,' I suddenly remembered. '*Zanto's* my name, not Z51!'

But Dr Allen didn't reply to that. Instead, she gave me a cardboard box with Z51 written on it in black marker pen. The she left.

I opened the box, and inside was my backpack, my Reygo shirt, my football boots, and—most precious—the metal torch that Dad had given me. I laughed, pulled on the shirt, and switched on my torch. The beam was weak, but it was there. It made me think of Dad and what he told me when he gave it to me.

'*You work hard and you try your best—that's why I'm proud of you every day.*'

I had to find him.

16

CAPO GREY

The next day I was feeling better, more like myself. I found a magazine with an article on Reygo.

'Brilliant!'

My reading was coming back slowly. I sat on my bed, tried a few words, but mostly looked at the pictures. I smoothed my hair and practised my Reygo poses.

The door opened and Dr Allen walked in. There was a man with her. He was short and chubby, wearing glasses, and dressed in a creased grey suit. He looked like a headmaster. His mouth was smiling, but his eyes weren't.

'This is Capo Grey, Commandant of the Island, Z51,' Dr Allen told me.

Dad told me to always be polite.

'Hello, how are you?' I said, and held out my hand.

'It can speak!' Capo Grey said. His voice was low and gentle, but not that friendly. 'Is it safe?' he asked the doctor.

'He's calm, I told you. He won't bite, will you Z51?'

'No, I prefer chocolate,' I said.

'But it's green,' Capo Grey said. 'Is it still a zombie?'

'Yes, but the mania has gone. It's almost like he's human again, only he has some elevated functions. He can see in the dark.'

It was true. It was like the vision I'd had in daylight when I was dead, seeing everything through dark red fuzzy glasses, was how I could see now at night. It was so cool, like a superpower! Plus, I was really strong. Capo Grey didn't seem impressed though.

'Give me your arm,' Capo Grey said to me.

I held it out, and he felt my wrist.

'Its flesh is warm, and it has a pulse. Amazing!' He dropped my arm. 'But are you 100% certain that the plan will work?'

'No, but we should try anyway,' the Doctor said. 'This is a *better* solution. He's as easy to control as any normal boy.'

'Boys are all delinquents,' the man shook his head. 'Very well, let's try to awake them all then. Now Z51…'

'My name's Zanto,' I told him.

'No dead creature in this camp has a name. You are Z51,' he said.

I stared at him in shock.

'But I'm alive now, and I do have a name. I'm Zanto!' I said.

Capo Grey stared at me with eyes like lasers. I knew I was in trouble.

'You need to learn a lesson, *Z51*,' he said. 'You are a zombie without a name! But, thanks to Dr Allen, you've been awoken, and now is not the time to cause trouble but rather to repay your debt.'

'Okay, how?' I asked. It seemed fair enough—they'd helped me.

'We don't know why, but your blood is special,' the doctor explained. 'It reacted with the antivirus and created a mutant protein that reversed the death and decay. If we take your blood, we can use it to make enough antidote protein to inject all the zombie kids on the Island. We hope that it will *awaken* them too.'

'Will it hurt?' I asked. I hated even thinking about blood, it made me feel ill. That was why I was a vegetarian

'No, it'll be just like having a jab,' Dr Allen said.

'But I hate jabs more than anything,' I said, feeling even greener.

'Afterward, you can eat as much chocolate as you like, to build your strength back up,' she said

Well, that was more tempting. Still, I wasn't too keen. Then I suddenly had a thought.

'Are *all* the infected kids who came here with me zombies now too?' I asked.

'Yes, you all turned,' Capo Grey nodded.

That meant that Nala was a zombie. I remembered how she'd wanted to be a doctor. I imagined her like I'd been, not having more than one simple thought, roaming across the camp and bouncing off the fences, screaming and snarling at the ordinary kids outside. I couldn't let her stay like that.

'Okay, I'll do it,' I said. 'But I want to choose which kid gets the medicine first.'

'I don't negotiate conditions with *inmates*,' Capo Grey said.

'Please! I'll do it anyway—I just want to help my friend first.'

He stared at me for what seemed like ages. Then at last he nodded.

'Very well, Z51. It seems that this is your chance to be a hero.'

When I'd lived in the Shambles, my idea of being a hero had been to play like Reygo and score for Real Magique, but my life had taken a different turn. Now, being a hero meant being jabbed for my blood to save zombies from brain death. I held out my arm to Dr Allen and she brought over a huge needle and pushed it towards my vein. I closed my eyes.

* * * *

I was standing at the fence with Dr Allen and two huge guards called Flint and Grimm. They didn't know me, but they seemed to hate me. Before we left the hospital, the guards sprayed a blue mist all over themselves. It smelled weird, like lavender and aniseed mixed.

'What's that?' I asked Dr Allen.

'Agent Blue,' she said. 'It seems to mask living human smell to the zombies, in case they need to go inside the fence. But it doesn't last long and doesn't work for all zombies. Some of the man-eaters will still attack.'

We were all looking into the Pen. It was strange. I could still remember the months I'd been inside looking out, not understanding anything, not really seeing anything. Now I was alive, outside and looking in at dead zombies.

'Do you see your friend?' Dr Allen asked.

I looked at the green faces, the snarling mouths, and the manic eyes of the zombies hurling themselves at the fence to try to reach us. Some of them were definitely man-eaters.

'No,' I said and kept searching.

There was a terrible smell, which I remembered from before I was a zombie, the stink of rotting flesh.

'We don't ever get used to your stench, green scum,'

Flint said to me holding his nose. I sniffed my armpits—I couldn't smell anything.

'Yeah, you stink like them, because you are one of them,' Grimm laughed.

'That's enough,' Dr Allen warned them.

I realised that I could smell Dr Allen, Flint, and Grimm too. It wasn't a hideous stench, like the dead, but they definitely smelled different to me. I wasn't sure how the dead zombies would react to me, now that I was alive again. Did I still smell like a zombie—could that be my disguise? I was curious.

I moved away from them and walked about ten metres along the fence. None of the frantic man-eaters followed me, they just kept hissing and scrambling to get at the 100% humans. Perhaps I was invisible to them? I walked back.

'I need to go inside and look for Nala,' I said.

'No, Z51, it's too dangerous. 'Dr Allen said. 'We only go in if there's an emergency, and then with water cannons and snipers. You're too valuable.'

The two guards snorted. They didn't think I was worth anything.

'I think I'll be fine,' I said. 'Look.'

I pushed my fingers through the fence, right in front of the zombies who looked the most furious and hungry.

They completely ignored me.

'See?' I said.

Grimm stepped forward and put his hand towards the fence. The zombies went berserk, slavering and gnashing their fangs to reach him. He stepped back fast.

'They know it's still one of them,' Grimm said pointing at me. 'It might work. Send it in, and if it's attacked, we'll shoot.'

I felt bad. I didn't want any zombie kids to be shot because of me. I knew that they couldn't help being what they were, but then I had to find Nala. Besides, I was pretty sure that I wouldn't be attacked.

I stood at the entrance to the Pen. There was a double gate, an outer, and an inner, with a small locked enclosure in the middle. The gates were controlled electronically.

'Are you ready, Z51?' Dr Allen asked.

There was a crowd of zombies on the other side. Flint and Grimm raised their rifles loaded with tranquiliser bullets and took aim.

'Ready!' I said.

Dr Allen pressed a button, the inner gate opened, and I walked into the Pen.

17

THE PEN

'Gnnarrragggh!'

A zombie was charging towards me.

'Z51, move out the way!' Grimm shouted. 'I've got no shot.'

'Gnnarrragggh!'

The zombie reached me and snarled in my face. His face was covered in yellow boils, and he had maggots feeding off his rancid flesh. I could smell his hideous breath, but I wasn't too scared, because I remembered this. All zombies would scream at each other. It didn't mean he was going to attack.

'Gnnarrragggh!' I screamed back at him, and he turned away and wandered off again. He was just saying hello. I walked on. Other zombies came up and screamed at me.

I yelled back and kept on moving, faster than they could keep up, searching for Nala.

It was strange seeing the Pen through normal eyes again. It was like some sort of barren hell—red mud trampled by the dragging feet of the zombies. They walked past me in different stages of decay, dead bits of flesh and skin hanging off, where they'd torn themselves on the barbed wire and not felt it. Some had big open wounds oozing with maggots. Others had yellow boils seeping pus down their faces. And the stench was beyond anything you could imagine, like walking through a brown swill of diarrhoea, pus, and rotting meat.

It was terrible standing there watching the zombie kids roam, pointless, hopeless, until their wasted legs could no longer hold up their mangled bodies. Then they just crawled. I looked into the eyes of every green kid that screamed in my face, or bounced off me. There was never any sign of a brain working inside their head, just a manic fury I knew they couldn't understand. And the worst, the very worst thing, was knowing that I'd been exactly like them only two weeks ago.

I wandered across the Pen. I was going to where a zombie girl with black braids used to watch me score goals against the fence. I heard a noise behind me and looked around. Something very weird was happening. There was a strange conga-line of about twenty lurching and staggering zombie kids following me. I turned to the nearest one.

'What do you want?' I asked her.

'Gnnarrragggh,' she cried and kept on lurching towards me.

Perhaps these zombies could smell that I was different to them now. What if I wasn't *invisible* after all? I looked at my 'fan-club' crawling and lurching through the mud after me. Perhaps they weren't my fans at all, but only hungry for my living flesh. By then, I was way out of reach of the guards with their guns. I walked faster.

'Gnnarrragggh,'

I felt something grab me from behind. I turned quick and pushed it away! The zombie staggered back and fell into the mud. It was Nala! Her manic red eyes glared at me. Her face had a couple of rotten holes, and her arms were covered in putrid boils. Her dark plaited braids were now more like dreadlocks near her skull. Her black talons were reaching for me and her yellow fangs yammered open and closed.

Surely, *she* couldn't be a man-eater? Not Nala. There was no evil in her heart, was there? I had to save her.

'Nala,' I crouched down. 'It's me—Zanto. I've come to make you better.'

'Gnnarrragggh!' she slavered at me.

'It's okay, I won't hurt you,' I offered her my hand and moved nearer.

'Gnnarrragggh!' she screamed, and her green hand shot forward and grabbed mine.

Nala started to pull me to her and she was so strong. Dr Allen had warned that the dead could be very powerful. She opened her jaws wide. But I realised she was using me to stand up. Still nervous, and with an eye on the other zombies, I pulled her up.

'Gnnarrragggh!' she screamed again, but then she stopped and seemed to calm down. I gripped her hand tight, and she returned my squeeze. She wasn't a man-eater! Somehow, she'd recognised me, and had wanted to come to me. She knew I was her friend. There was something left of Nala inside her.

'Come on!'

I stepped forward, and she managed to stagger along next to me. But now we were surrounded on all sides by the mud-splattered hoard. Had they come to attack, or just to scream hello and be part of the gang? My heart was beating so hard it hurt. I didn't want to die again.

But the zombies didn't attack. Instead, they just seemed curious, like they didn't know what I was. Still, it was time for me to get out of there. I pulled Nala forward, and she turned back to them and screamed at the hoard, but they kept following us.

Suddenly, a huge zombie with a Mohican haircut appeared. It had a half-eaten rat in its hands and blood dripping down its face. It was sniffing the air, looking for the source of the smell. Then it turned its bulging red eyes to me and threw down the rat. This one was definitely a man-eater and thought I smelled like dinner! It charged.

I grabbed Nala by the hand—it was ice cold—and raced to the exit with the Mohican in hot pursuit. It was snarling in rage. I could see the gates, but didn't think we'd make it as Nala's dead zombie legs couldn't run that fast.

'Open the gates!' I yelled. They started to open.

'Faster, Z51!' Doctor Allen called.

The Mohican hurled itself at me through the air.

Thud.

It fell into the mud. It had been taken out by Flint with his tranquiliser gun. We made it out of the Pen and the gates closed behind us. We were safe.

* * * *

I was in the hospital with Nala. She didn't mind me coming near her, but she screamed at the humans who'd never been infected. She hissed and snarled and tried to swipe any nurse who came near. I knew she was just scared. I helped Flint and Grimm strap her onto the bed.

She wasn't happy about that. She spat and screamed.

'It's okay,' I told her. 'They won't hurt you.'

I held her hand, but she glared and growled at me. Then Dr Allen injected her with the medicine.

Nala thrashed around like she was being electrocuted. Then she screamed like she was in terrible pain and collapsed onto the bed, unconscious, her eyelids closed over her wild red pupils. She looked like she was truly, permanently dead.

'Is she okay?' I looked at Dr Allen.

She picked up Nala's wrist and held it. She waited for what seemed like a year, and then she smiled.

'Feel for yourself,' she said.

I put my fingers over Nala's wrist and I felt her pulse. She was warm. She was alive again!

18

PRISONERS

The next day, Nala opened her eyes. They were still red but not angry anymore, just tired and confused. She couldn't speak, and she was only awake for a few minutes. While she slept, the nurses picked the maggots out of her wounds, stitched them up, and painted antiseptic lotion on her boils. Dr Allen said that Nala's body needed to rest and heal.

There were other kids in the hospital who they'd awoken too, but not many. Dr Allen said that they had to go slowly because they didn't have that much medicine, or enough staff to watch the patients. By *watch* they meant tie them down and station armed guards—no one was taking any risks.

The next day they brought in Ginga-Nut and I

recognised him. For some reason, since I'd awoken, I'd completely forgotten about him. I watched them bring him back to life too. That was all good. But the worse thing for me was that every two days they took more of my blood, to grow the mutated antibodies.

Some days Nala was awake, but she was scared and confused. She'd hide under her bedclothes if I came near her. I noticed that, like me, she was growing black scabs over her nasty sores. Dead zombies never had scabs, only dripping wounds. By then, my skin was a paler shade of green and completely healed. When Nala's scabs fell off, she'd be the same. It took two weeks for her to wake up properly. I went in one day, and she was sitting cross-legged on her bed. She looked at me and wasn't scared. Her eyes were still a bit red, but the pupils were black again.

'Zaaannntttoooo!' she said and smiled.

Her teeth were like mine, more yellow and pointier than a 100% human's, but not massive dripping fangs.

Dr Allen ran lots of test on Nala and, like me, she could see in the dark and was strong. But sadly, she also couldn't read much anymore. It bothered her way more than it had me, because she'd always been so clever. Over the next few weeks, while I was still on the simple ABC books, Nala re-learned how to read again, fast. Only problem was, she'd forgotten most of the stuff she'd learned from all those years at school.

* * * *

Three months later, and Nala was still trying to relearn everything that she used to know.

'We need a school here,' she said to Dr Allen.

'Capo Grey won't allow it,' the doctor said.

'But surely even zombie kids have a right to learn and go to school?' Nala replied.

'You'll have to ask Capo Grey,' Dr Allen said.

We asked to see him. While we waited for him to reply, Nala read anything she could find, and I played football with a new ball that the nurses had bought for me.

Most days I'd be in the yard near the hospital kicking my football against a brick wall, practising my Beckham-bend around an imaginary defence. I'd tried to put a soccer team together, but it was too hard because most of the Awoken were still completely rubbish at every-thing. It took all their energy just to walk—no way could they dribble or kick. G-Nut used to be good at football, but now he was obsessed with moonwalking. Only he hadn't quite managed to get control of his legs yet, and he kept falling onto his backside. Still, it didn't bother him—he'd stand back up again and carry on.

Nala was pretty slick on her feet, but all she wanted

to do all day was practice UFC and read. She was useless at football. Some days she'd take pity on me and go in goal, because she could actually catch a ball, even if she couldn't kick one.

Each day, Nala helped me read a little bit more of the magazine article on Reygo. He'd come from a poor background, just like us. He'd been born on an island, and his dad was a gardener like mine. He'd gone to the Mainland and become the greatest footballer in the world. I was going to do that too, whether I was green or not. But, for now, I wasn't going anywhere.

The Awoken kids lived in tents, with separate dorms for the boys and girls. In the centre of the enclosure was a big mess tent where we ate and had books, games, a computer, and a TV. There were about two hundred of us in the hospital grounds. Half of them couldn't remember who they'd been before they'd died. The ones who could remember told us their names, like Jens, Dolph, and Greta. They were the three blonde kids I'd seen when we first got put in the tent in the Third State. And there was Ben, Obi, Nazlah, and Julio, too. We'd all escaped from the Shambles, or the Iron City.

We called the ones who didn't know their names by the number they had on their wrists, like Z22, Z533, or Z75. We still had our bands too—Jack was Z53, and Nala was Z52. We needed to know our numbers because the guards, doctors, and nurses only ever called us by those. Like Capo Grey had told me, no one on the Island was allowed a name. Names were for real humans, and we Awoken were just zombies to them.

But whether we had names or not, at least an Awoken could stay in the hospital compound. We were the lucky ones. The medicine hadn't worked for the others, and their hearts and brains never restarted. Those poor dudes were put back into the Pen, doomed to stay dead forever. We called the manic dead zombies the DeeZees. The folk who had always been human, and *never dead*, like Dr Allen and the nurses, we called the N-Deds.

The Pen was right next door to our enclosure. I could see the DeeZees roaming around, screaming and snarling, their flesh rotting, and their skin still covered in boils. Dr Allen didn't know if our *cure* was permanent. I was freaked out to think we might return to being DeeZees again.

One dark night, I was in my tent watching the moths flying around with my night vision and hearing mozzies whine. I switched on my torch and thought about Dad. Where was he? Did he think I was dead? The beam was low, but still alive. I hadn't given up hope of seeing him again. I was determined that somehow, I'd get out of that prison.

19

VISITORS AND HOPE

Obi had become our leader. He was the kind of guy I'd have swapped Romeo for any day. He was about seventeen and really big and strong, like a rugby or NFL player. He had worked out to get fit again, and his shrivelled zombie flesh had transformed back into muscle. Even being locked up all day didn't seem to get him down. He was the most cheerful of us all.

'When I get free, I'm going to join the army,' he told us. 'Be in the special forces like my dad was.'

I reckoned he'd get there too, so long as they let zombies into the army. He loved to talk about his future, his dreams. While we sat in the mess before lights-out, he'd make up adventure tales for us, and it was better than TV. In his stories, he was always the hero and could escape from the unlikeliest situation. He was so cool! We all loved him, like you love the best player on your team. He was our captain.

One very hot day, we were all in the yard outside the mess tent. Some of the Awoken girls had dressed-up from a box of fancy dress stuff and face-paint the nurses had given them. They'd transformed their green faces into a N-Ded colour again with pinky-white, or brown paint, and they did look almost *normal*. Whatever *that* was for us now. I was playing keepy-uppy. I was at 76 *ups*, and not nearly tired yet.

'I'm so bored!' Nala yelled out and threw her book down onto the dirt. 'I've read the same book four times,' she stood up and stamped about the yard. 'Bored, bored, bored, bored, bored!'

'What's up?' Obi asked.

'I want some new books, and a laptop, and the Internet. How can I learn like this? I want to go to school!' she yelled.

'She's a nutter,' G-Nut said, mid moon-dance.

'Look who's talking, you dancing Lamebrain!' Nala shouted. 'Argg!' she screamed and ran away around the corner of the hospital.

'I'll go talk to her,' Obi said.

'No, it's alright—I'll do it,' I said.

'Tell her everything will be okay,' he said. 'She's got to chill out for now, but think of the future. Dream the biggest dream she can. It *will* come true if she truly believes it—if she has hope!'

Nala ran to the far end of our enclosure, and I followed her. For once, the manic DeeZees in the Pen next door were quiet. We weren't supposed to hang around near them because we upset them, like the N-Deds did. Over time, we must have smelled more like N-Deds and less like zombies, because the DeeZees got agitated when we were close. And more of the man-eaters, like Mohican dude, acted like they wanted to eat us too. We weren't *invisible* any more.

Nala leapt onto the high fence with barbed wire on top that separated us from the outside world, gripping on with her green fingers and black nails. There were some N-Ded kids on the outside, playing five-aside football on a small dirt pitch about fifty metres away. I guessed they were same ones I'd screamed at when I was a DeeZee. I knew by then that they were kids from the local village. Our prison backed onto their park, but they never came near enough for us to talk to them. Too scared of us, I guess, or afraid of being infected. I doubt if they noticed we were different to the screaming green DeeZees next door in the Pen.

'Hey, you lot, N-Deds, I'm bored!' Nala yelled at them and rattled the fence. 'Come over and talk to us.'

But they couldn't hear her and carried on playing. The guard Flint walked up and ordered her to get down.

'What if I don't?' Nala said. 'Will you shoot me? I'm a zombie already, and I've got no life here, so what do I care?'

'Just get down,' he said.

'Okay, there you go!' Nala said and let go of the fence. She landed on her back in the red dirt and just lay there.

'Get back to the yard,' Flint said. 'I'll be back to check up on you soon.'

He walked off, and Nala just laughed.

'He'll ground us to our tents. You'd better get up,' I said.

'Why?' she replied, and stayed there, staring up at the sun. 'Capo Grey won't see us, won't help us, and no one from the Mainland even knows we're alive again. Nothing's ever going to change.'

Outside the fence, a van drove up onto the pitch—it had a satellite dish on its roof, and '*Channel One*' written on the side. It stopped where the boys were playing. A TV crew climbed out, with a kid about my age and size, and the same black hair. He was wearing a full replica Reygo kit. He started kicking his football in keepy-uppy, while the TV crew spoke to the kids on the pitch. He was pretty good.

I walked up to the fence and pressed my face against it, trying to hear what they were saying, but they were too far away. There was a reporter lady with a microphone interviewing them.

They must have asked the local kids to show off their soccer skills because three of them starting playing keepy-uppy for the camera. They were *useless*. Replica Kit Dude shook his head and took the ball back off them. He tried passing to them, and they all fired at the goal—and missed. Replica Kit Dude faced the camera and put his thumb down. The reporter lady shrugged her shoulders. I recognised her. She was called Sally Singson and was very famous in the United Republic.

I gave a loud whistle, and Sally and the kids looked over. I threw the football up and caught it on the back of my neck; then I let it drop onto my foot. I kicked the ball high again, did a header, and then bounced it onto my knee. I could keep these tricks going for ages. When I looked over again, the film crew was walking towards us. Replica Kit Dude and the local boys were following be-hind. They all looked nervous—they probably thought we were man-eaters.

'Hey Nala,' I said, keeping my eyes on the ball. 'Sally Singson's out there.'

'Here on the Island. Why?' I heard her jump to her feet.

'Don't know, but are they filming me?' I asked, as the ball bounced off my knee—I was at 26 'ups.'

'Looks like it,' she said.

I kicked the ball up high again, did a backwards somersault, and caught it before I landed. Sally clapped. I gave a bow and smoothed my hair into Reygo perfection. Replica Kit Dude was staring at me like I wasn't even human.

There were two fences between us, so they couldn't get too close. But Sally was near enough to talk to us. She was looking at us with screwed-up eyes, curious. The cameraman was filming.

'Hi there, Sally,' Nala said.

They all jumped in shock—actually up into the air! Nala and I laughed. Sally pressed her face against the fence.

'You can *speak*?' she asked.

'Well, *yeah*, I just did,' Nala said.

'We can all talk in here,' I said. 'We're called the *Awoken* because we came alive again.' I turned to the Replica Kit Dude. 'Are you looking for soccer players, because I can play, really well?'

But he never replied. Instead, they all just stared at us like we were talking Russian.

'Did you get all that?' Sally asked the cameraman.

'Yep,' he said.

'Keep the camera rolling,' Sally said. 'This is the story of a lifetime.'

She turned back to us, holding out her microphone.

'So, what are your names, kids?' she asked.

We told her.

'And you guys are *zombies*, right?' Sally asked.

'Well, yeah!' I laughed. 'We're green with yellow fangs,' I said and showed my pointy teeth.

'And you *died*?'

'Of course, we did,' Nala replied. 'But we came back to life because of Zanto's mutated blood.'

'Could you tell me more?' Sally asked.

'Well,' I began, 'it all started because of *my* higher brain function.'

'Here we go again—stop bragging!' Nala interrupted. 'Sally, can you ask Il Presido to let us out of this prison?' she asked. 'Because I want to be a doctor, only we don't have a school.

'And is there any specialisation that interests you?' Sally asked.

'Genetics for sure. I want to study how the zombie mutation affects our genes. Only four letters make up each DNA code – and a variation is called an SNP. Just imagine – it could be only one letter wrong in our code that turned us into zombies. What if I could find that and fix it?'

'Why are you here? Did you like my skills?' I asked Replica Kit Dude, but he still didn't answer.

'I thought you were amazing, Zanto,' Sally smiled at me. 'We're on the Island, because Il Presido wants everyone to focus on the future, not on what we've lost. He's announced that in a month's time we'll have the Hope Games in the Capital. It's a sports competition for children from all around the world, because they are the future.'

'What, like an Olympic Games for kids?' Nala asked.

'Kind of,' Sally nodded. 'This is Zack Starr,' she pointed at Replica Kit Dude. 'He's going to every town looking for the best players for the United Republic Boys Soccer team. He's the Captain.'

'What about a girls' team?' Nala asked.

'That's another film crew with the girls' Captain,' Sally said.

'Humph,' Nala replied, unconvinced it was fair.

'Hey—I can be on your soccer team!' I yelled at Zack.

'Well, you're the best player we've seen all week, isn't he Zack?' Sally said.

He didn't answer. I had to convince him.

'Yeah—I'm brilliant. Watch this.'

I rolled the ball onto my foot, up onto my knee then kicked it high, and over my head and through a basketball hoop that was on the wall behind me.

'He shoots, he scores,' I laughed. 'I never miss. I'm pretty much always the best player on the pitch. If you pick me, we'll win for sure.'

Zack scowled.

'He's the best at bragging too,' Nala laughed. I smiled, I didn't mind.

'You have to talk to Capo Grey and tell him you need me for the team,' I said to Zack. But he stared at us like we were just talking zombies and nothing more.

'Perhaps Zack can help,' Sally said. 'Il Presido is his uncle.' She turned to him. 'What do you say, Zack?'

'Are you insane?' Zack yelled at last. 'How can *that one* be a doctor? Or *this one* be on *my* United Republic Boys' Soccer team? They're green—they're dead—they stink—they're *zombies*! They're not even humans. They should be stamped on like... like... like *cockroaches!*'

He stormed off back to their TV truck.

What he said about us made me feel sick. Was that what we were now—cockroaches?

'What a loser,' Nala growled. 'I'm going to get that kid one day.'

'Never mind him, kids,' Sally said to us. 'When the people see your skills on the news tonight, Zanto, they'll want you on the team even if you're a zombie.

You'll see.'

I liked Sally.

'And Nala, when they see how clever you are, and hear that you want to be a doctor, no one will be able to keep you locked up in here in prison—children have rights. Now, about your mutated blood, Zanto. How exactly were you guys *Awoken*?'

But, before we could answer, there was a huge commotion outside the fence. Two prison trucks raced up. The guards, led by Grimm and Flint, jumped out and surrounded the film crew.

'You're on restricted ground,' Grimm said. 'No more questions.'

'But this is public property,' Sally said. 'I'm just talking to the kids here.'

'No more filming,' Flint said. 'Z51 and Z52, get back to the yard.'

'Hey, these kids have names!' Sally said.

'Not here they don't,' Grimm replied. 'You shouldn't be here—it's not safe.'

'They're just kids,' Sally protested.

That's when the screaming and snarling howled up from the Pen, which was only about five metres away. I guess the DeeZees had woken up and smelled the N-Deds. The man-eaters were hurling themselves at the fence, screeching, and yammering their huge fangs together. The boys ran off to a safe distance, and Sally and her crew looked sacred.

'None of these kids are tame,' Grimm said. 'They're all zombies, like them.' He pointed his gun at the Pen. Then he turned to us. 'You two clear off. Or you'll be grounded in your tents for a year.'

Nala scowled and swore under her breath, but she knew we had to go. We never saw what happened to Sally Singson and her crew.

20

IN TROUBLE

That night we sat in the mess. There was only one TV. We wanted to watch the news, but a couple of bigger boys tried to stop us. Nala was ready for a fight, as usual.

'Just let them watch their show,' Obi stepped in.

Everyone always obeyed him. He was the biggest, but luckily for the smaller kids, also the fairest. We switched to the news.

'Boring!' G-Nut yelled and flicked his plastic plate at the TV.

'Shut up and watch,' Nala said to him. 'Even your one lonely brain cell might learn something.'

I guess those two would never be friends, dead or alive.

'Nice one,' Obi gave her a high five.

The news seemed all good. The Infection was contained, and the Iron City was locked down. There was a lot of talk about the Hope Games, and then—the best news ever! Reygo was going to be in the United Republic for the boys' and girls' soccer finals. He was a Goodwill Ambassador. He was the one who was going to present the Cuppa to the winners.

I knew then that it was my destiny. I was going to be in the United Republic team, win the soccer tournament, and meet Reygo. I had a dream again! Once Sally showed my skills to the nation, everyone would want me on the team. I could hardly concentrate for the rest of the show. At last, right at the end, came Sally Singson's report.

'This is it guys, Nala and me being interviewed,' I cried. 'We're going to be famous!' All the other Awoken payed attention.

The film showed Sally on the Island with the kids on the soccer pitch doing their rubbish keepy-uppy.

'It's us next,' Nala said. 'Capo Grey will have to give us a school now!'

The film went to the Captain, Zack Starr, talking to the camera.

'We toured the whole of the Island,' he said, *'but we didn't see anyone with skills good enough for the United Republic team. No one near as good as me. It was so disappointing. I don't know where we're going to find players good enough.'*

He smiled at the camera.

'I'm going to get that idiot!' Nala said.

'I can't stand that kid,' Obi said. 'Sorry, Zanto.' He put his hand on my shoulder. 'I know you're good enough.'

'No, it's okay,' I said. 'Because when Sally shows my skills, the whole country will see how well I play...'

But there was no clip of my keepy-uppy, because the film ended right there. There wasn't one shot of the zombie prison, and not one mention of us. No one knew that we existed, that we were Awoken, or could play football, or wanted a school.

'Captain Zero and Miss Loser,' G-Nut flicked my ear. 'Turn the channel back to something decent.'

'But why didn't Sally show our interview?' I asked. 'I thought she wanted to help us.'

'Because we're zombies.' Nala said. 'You heard that creep Zack—they'd rather squash us like cockroaches.'

'Come on, we'll be fine!' Obi said. 'One day soon we'll get out of here, just focus on that.'

Grimm came into the mess.

'You two troublemakers, Z51 and Z52, Capo Grey wants to see you. Time to pay for misbehaving.'

* * * *

We were taken out of the yard, through the electric gates, Grimm and Flint on each side of us. I stumbled.

'Keep up, you green scum,' Flint hissed.

Nala glared at him. I shook my head at her—she was always too brave for her own good. We came to a dark concrete building and they took us inside. We passed a control room with lots of cameras showing the Awoken kids in the yard and the hospital. There were silent videos playing of the manic screams of the DeeZees in the Pen. They made me shiver. I was scared that one day I might be like them again—lost in a dark and confused red mist like before.

'This way,' Grimm said.

We walked down a long corridor with just one light bulb hanging on a wire. The guards' boots echoed off the concrete floor. At the end was a plain door with '*Capo Grey*' written on it. Flint banged on it.

'Z51 and Z52 here, sir,' he called.

'Send them in,' Capo Grey replied. He sounded bored.

We walked in. Grimm and Flint waited outside. Capo Grey looked just like I remembered him, dressed in a creased suit, and wearing glasses. He was leaning back in a leather chair behind a desk with vase of flowers on it, and there was a picture of Il Presido on the wall behind him. He had the fingers of both hands joined at the tips like he was making a church. He didn't seem angry, but he wasn't smiling either, just staring at us over the top of his glasses. It was exactly like going to the headmaster.

Of course, Nala couldn't keep her mouth shut.

'I need books!' she blurted out.

Capo Grey raised an eyebrow.

'You have books,' he said.

'They're for little kids.'

'I'll think about it.'

'Can I have a laptop too?' I thought she was pushing it.

'Why?' Capo Grey asked.

'So I can catch up on my classes. Or perhaps, I can go to the school in the village?'

'Not possible, I'm afraid,' Capo Grey replied.

'Then can we have a school in here?' Nala wasn't giving up. 'I need to learn all my maths and science again.'

Was she mad? Who'd volunteer for maths?

'But why do you need to learn? To what end?' Capo Grey opened his hands.

'So that I can go to college,' Nala said. 'I want to be a doctor.'

'But there's no university on the Island,' he shrugged. 'So how can you be a doctor?'

'I'll go to college on the Mainland, in the Capital City, like the other kids,' Nala said.

Capo Grey laughed, but he didn't sound like he thought it was funny.

'Il Presido has decreed that all zombie orphans be cared for on the Island. This is your home now. And to take care of you is *my* noble duty.'

'But *I'm* not an orphan,' I said. 'I think my dad's in the Capital City. If he is, Nala and I can go live with him. He'd help her go to college.'

'Was your father from the Shambles?' Capo Grey asked me.

'Yeah.'

'Then he'll be in one of the camps for the displaced without visas, and not allowed to work. You'll be better cared for here,' he said. That made me angry.

'But he's my dad!' I cried. 'I want to be with him.'

'And I want to go to school!' Nala yelled.

'And I want to be in the Hope Games,' I said. 'I reckon I could get into the soccer team. But I have to go the Mainland.'

'Enough!' Capo Grey banged his hand down on his desk and stood up. He leaned forward over the table and glared down at us. 'I must protect the people and borders of our United Republic. Do you know how I do that?'

'Not really...' Nala said.

'By keeping all *zombies* quarantined on this Island. Your vile Infection mustn't spread.'

'But *we're* not infectious any more,' I said. 'We're Awoken.'

'Look at you, Z51! You're a zombie—you're not human anymore.'

'How can you say that?' Nala cried. 'Of course we're human. We're just normal kids with green skin.'

'Even if I believed that,' Capo Grey shook his head, 'the people outside that gate won't. You won't be safe out there. Frightened people will attack you before you attack them.'

'But Il Presido can order them to leave us alone, protect us,' Nala said. 'We don't want to hurt anyone.'

Capo Grey sighed and sat down again.

'I won't take that risk with your safety. You don't need to go to college, Z52, because you'll never be a doctor. Which hospital would ever let *you* near its vulnerable patients? You'll stay on the Island and be protected *forever*...'

What? I felt a hot pain in my head. *Forever* was a long time.

'No way!' I yelled.

'We want to leave *now*!' Nala said.

Capo Grey paused and smiled. 'Well...I suppose I could send you to the Iron City, then,' he replied.

'But it's overrun with zombies,' Nala said.

'Well, you *are* zombies just like them,' Capo Grey smiled again.

'But we're not the same anymore,' I said. 'We're *Awoken*'.

'The man-eaters know we're different—they'll attack us,' Nala said.

'I agree. So, to be *safe*, you must remain here on the Island,' Capo Grey opened his hands like he was being kind. 'Along with all the other...*creatures* out there.'

'But it's not right to keep us locked up when we haven't done anything wrong,' Nala said.

'That's not true,' Capo Grey said. 'You've committed crimes.'

'What *crimes*?' I asked.

'On orders of Il Presido, no citizens were allowed to travel to the Third State without a visa. But *you* did, which makes you illegal immigrants.'

'But we *had* to come,' I said. 'The zombies overran the Shambles.'

'And it was bombed,' Nala said.

'But you paid a *gangster* to smuggle you into the Third State,' Capo Grey said. 'That's a crime too.'

'But we *had* to pay him, or he wouldn't let us escape,' I explained.

'I didn't make these laws, which you've broken, Z51. I merely obey the orders of Il Presido. Criminals are not rewarded with a visa to the Mainland—they stay on the Island.'

'But I need to go to the Capital City and find my dad,' I said. 'You have to let me go.'

Capo Grey stared at me.

'Do you think I'll risk one citizen being devoured by you, Z51?'

'But I've never eaten anyone. I'm a vegetarian!' I cried.

'Any zombie could turn cannibal—we take no risks.'

'But not all zombies are bad,' I said. 'Some just want to feed kids, or eat ice cream, or get their catapult, or, or, or...*play football*. I still just want to play football, and I can't do that here.'

'Zombies playing football—ridiculous! You may be an *Awoken*, Z51, but that doesn't stop you being dangerous. None of you kids will ever go to the Mainland. And don't think that Sally Singson can help you. I've told her that if she tells anyone you Awoken exist, she'll be sent to prison, too—for revealing government secrets. No one will ever know you're here. Now leave!'

When we got back to the mess, we were both in despair. Nala didn't say a word, but I saw tears rolling down her green cheeks. What was the point of being Awoken, and of feeling like a real live human again, if that life was trapped forever on the Island, with no hope of escape? And no chance of any future that we wanted to live? To never be a doctor. To never be in special forces. To never have a chance of seeing your dad. To never play football.

I sank down in the corner of my tent and covered my eyes with my hands. I didn't cry, but I was close. I tried to think of something happy, something real outside that prison. I tried to remember how Reygo moved when he ran towards the goal. I used to copy his every move, but now I couldn't remember them. Everything inside my head had gone black. I couldn't even dream anymore.

21

HOPELESS

Everyone in the yard was now depressed. They'd heard the news that we'd never be allowed to leave the Island. For the whole of the next day, Nala didn't say a single word but sat on her own, with her arms wrapped round her knees. The next morning, she was sitting at a table in the mess, reading a massive book.

'What's that?' I asked.

'A book on biology that Dr Allen gave me,' she said. 'I'll need to understand it if I'm going to be a doctor.'

'What's the point? Capo Grey says you'll never go to college,' I reminded her.

'I'm not giving up,' she said. 'My dream will come true one day.'

She was tougher than me. I couldn't find any way of seeing the future any more. But I wasn't as bad as Obi.

He'd always been the strongest of us, always the happiest, but the news he'd never leave this prison had flipped a switch inside him. The laughter left his eyes, and he stopped working out, stopped telling stories of his fantasy army adventures, and worst, he stopped smiling. Instead, he just sat cross-legged near the fence in the rain and stared longingly at the world outside, which he could never be a part of. Nala tried to get him to eat, but he wouldn't.

'Obi, remember you can still have big dreams,' she told him.

'My dream was Special Forces,' he replied, quietly. 'Even if I do get out of here in a few years, it'll be too late for me.'

He stayed there for three days, and then Nala and I went to fetch Dr Allen. She took Obi to the hospital. But he could hardly walk, and was staggering like a DeeZee.

'Is he tired?' Nala asked.

'I hope that's all it is, Z52,' Dr Allen said. 'His pulse is very slow.' She looked worried.

Obi was in hospital for a week. I don't remember much about those seven days, other giving up practising football. Instead, I lay on my back in the tent staring up at canvas, listening to raindrops, and counting mosquitoes. Nala tried to make me go out for a walk, even tried to kick the football at me, but what was the point? Dr

Allen came to ask if she could take more of my blood—she said it was an emergency. I couldn't even be bothered to answer. I just shrugged and followed her to the clinic. What did I care?

I sat on the hospital bed. It was the same one I'd awoken in, so many months ago. The room in which I'd first remembered what life was, what my dreams were, before they'd been taken away again. There was a newspaper on the table. I recognised the kid on the front page. It was Zack Starr, Captain of the United Republic Boys' team. He was standing with the team, boasting how he was the best player, ready to win the Hope Games.

'I can't stand that kid,' Dr Allen said.

I didn't reply. She put the needle into my vein. I didn't even flinch this time. I didn't care that it hurt me. She took the blood.

'You look very sad, Zanto,' Dr Allen said. It was the first time she'd used my real name. I just shrugged.

'I'm sorry that you're here, you know. But there's nothing I can do. I'm not allowed to tell anyone what happens on the Island.'

No point in me saying anything. A nurse came racing in.

'Come quickly, Doctor, were losing him!' she said.

The two of them ran out into the corridor.

That made me curious. I climbed off the bed and followed them. They disappeared into a room two doors down. I walked down the corridor and looked in through the window. What I saw made my scalp shrink tight with fright. It was Obi, but not Awoken Obi, as I knew him, green but still handsome, laughing and strong, looking after the small kids, making sure we were all okay. Not Obi who smiled so that you could just see the tips of his sharp pale-yellow teeth, as he told his daft stories.

This was a DeeZee Obi strapped to the bed, a putrid shade of green, his eyes furious red and glaring, and his long yellow fangs dripping with spit. His twisted long black talons were trying to swipe the nurses. He was lost to that dreadful dark red zombie mist again! It was so sad, and so *scary*.

Flint and Grimm came charging up the corridor, their boots hammering. I stepped out of the way and they crashed into the treatment room. Dr Allen injected Obi with medicine, but he still kept thrashing around. She took out another needle and injected him again. That time he fell asleep.

Dr Allen came out and stood by my side. We watched as the guards wheeled Obi away on a trolley. He'd been the big brother I'd always wished for, instead of that bully Romeo.

'What's happened to him?' I asked.

'I don't know,' the doctor admitted. 'His pulse kept slowing down until, at last, it was so slow we could hardly feel it. There was nothing we could do.'

'So, has he died again?' I asked.

'I don't think so. But somehow his heart got so slow that the zombie mutation took control once more. If I didn't know that such things are impossible, I'd say he has a broken heart.'

'Last year zombies were impossible,' I said.

'Yes. But he was such a lovely boy,' Dr Allen was crying. 'It's so unfair.'

She was right—it was unfair.

'Surely, there's some hope?' I said. 'Can't you give him the medicine from my blood again?'

'I tried, but it didn't work this time.'

'Where are they taking him?' I asked.

'To the Pen,' Dr Allen said. 'He's too dangerous to stay here'.

I could tell you that was the moment I lost all hope, but perhaps it had gone already.

Back in my hospital room, Dr Allen locked the door behind her.

'Zanto, I have to tell you something,' she said quietly. 'But you must promise not to tell anyone, not even Z52.'

'What?' I didn't care what it was.

'I didn't actually pick you from the Pen because you

had a higher brain function; it was because the guards were concerned you were getting the other zombies too excited. They wanted you gone, so I used you for my experiment.'

'Oh.' I was disappointed and embarrassed. 'But I thought you wanted someone who seemed brighter, so you could try to awaken them with your new drug?'

'Oh, Zanto...' She looked guilty. 'We weren't trying to cure you. We were...' She stopped.

'You were what?'

'We were trying to find a way a way to neutralise you, *forever*. We injected you with a serum that we thought was strong enough, but it had the opposite effect and brought you back to life.'

I stepped back from her.

'You tried to *kill* me?' I cried.

'That was before I knew you, Zanto, before I learned that not all zombies are evil,' she said. 'You kids aren't here on the Island because Capo Grey wants to protect you. You're here because he's still searching for a way to destroy the zombies in the Iron City. We're using your blood to develop a new mutation—a weapon. I want to stop, but he won't let me. And that's why he'll never allow you to leave here. He knows you aren't infectious or dangerous, but the Awoken are too valuable to our research now.'

'And what happens if you find a weapon? Will Capo

Grey use it on us? Will he neutralise the Awoken too?'

'I don't know, Zanto,' she said. 'I'm so sorry.'

What use was her being sorry?

'So, don't help him!' I yelled.

'I have to,' she said. 'I'm under orders, and there's nothing I can do.'

'So why tell me?' I asked.

'To ask you to forgive me...'

I stared at her. Had she lost her mind?

'No, I don't forgive you!' I cried. 'If you don't help me, it's your fault too!'

I didn't tell the others in The Yard. There was no point them feeling as bad as I did. Besides, they already felt terrible enough because we'd all loved Obi like our big brother and we'd lost him.

22

GiVING UP

A fortnight passed, and I hardly did anything. I lay in my hot tent squashing bugs, or else in the mess, watching Nala reading and G-Nut moonwalking. At night, I stared at the inside of the tent with my red vision. I think I'd forgotten all about my dad at that point. And I never once thought of Reygo. One night, I took out my torch and switched it on, but the battery was dead. I couldn't remember who'd given it to me. I dropped it on the floor, and it rolled under my cot.

I sat near the fence and looked out all day, like Obi had done. I saw the boys outside playing football and didn't even remember that the Hope Games were taking place. Nala sat down next to me, near the fence.

'I found your torch, Zanto,' she said. 'You must have lost it in the tent.'

So what, who cared?

'I got some batteries from Dr Allen,' she said. 'See, it works again.' She switched it on and shone the light in my face. I growled at her, it hurt my eyes.

'Here,' she gave it to me.

I just put it in my pocket. She frowned at me.

'Your dad gave you that, remember?' she asked. I shrugged.

She took hold of my wrist.

'Your pulse is getting slower, Zanto,' she said. 'You have to fight this!'

I didn't know what she meant.

'Remember your dreams. Tell me about Reygo,' she said.

'Who's Reygo?' I asked.

'Are you serious? Only the best footballer in the world. Perhaps you'll meet him one day…'

I couldn't be bothered to reply. I watched a fly buzzing.

'Zanto! Don't give up! Because if your heart breaks, you'll be a DeeZee again, and they'll send you back to the Pen! They sent Greta there yesterday—she was screaming and snarling.'

But I didn't care. I just wanted to sleep.

I was jolted awake by the sound of three huge trucks driving up the dirt road that led to the prison. The gates opened and the trucks rumbled in. They drove towards the Pen. Nala took my hand.

'Come on, let's go see what that's about,' she said.

I couldn't be bothered.

'Zanto, get your lazy backside off the dirt!' she yelled at me. 'And man up!' She yanked my arm.

'Okay, chill out,' I said and dragged myself up. It took all my energy to put one foot in front of the other. It was like I could feel the DeeZee dark red mist covering me already.

'Come on,' Nala dragged me after her.

We reached the Pen's fence and pressed our faces against its wire. Soldiers were rounding up some of the screaming DeeZee kids, using what looked like laser guns. They shone the beams at the zombies' faces, and the DeeZees hated it so much they staggered away. They were herding them, like dogs move sheep, into the trucks. When these were full, Flint and Grimm locked the tailgates, and the convoy drove away down the road, red dirt clouding behind them. There were still around a thousand zombies left in the Pen.

'What do you reckon that was about?' Nala asked.

'Don't know,' I said. I didn't care either.

'Listen!' Nala instructed.

We were standing just behind Flint and another guard, but they didn't see us.

'How long before they get to the Mainland?' The other guard asked.

'Four hours,' Flint said. 'Grimm and Capo Grey are there to meet them. There'll be more trucks arriving tomorrow for the last batch.' And then they walked away.

'Zanto, did you hear that? They're moving some DeeZees to the Mainland,' Nala said. Her hands were on my shoulders. 'Zanto? Zanto, liven up!'

But I didn't hear anything else she said.

That night when I lay down on my bunk, the flies crawled on my face. I knew if my heart slowed down too much, I'd turn back into a raving DeeZee. I held my wrist, but could hardly feel any pulse. I didn't want to be lost in the red mist again, but I didn't have the energy to care. I had no hope to stay awake for, and recently I hadn't even dreamt in my sleep anymore.

Only that night was different, because I did!

I was in the Crystal Stadium and it was full, surrounded on all sides by a waving crowd. I was in a football team of N-Deds, and they were screaming at me and pointing forward. And then I realised there was a ball at my feet. I tried to move, only I couldn't feel my legs. I looked to where the players were pointing and saw the goal at the far end of the pitch, but ten opposition players stood between me and the net. It was too hard. I was going to just sit down and go to sleep. Then I felt a hand on my shoulder. I turned, and he was there—Reygo, standing right beside me!

'Time to wake up, Zanto. The game's not over yet,' he said. 'You need a goal, and there's only one minute left. The team needs you. You can do it.'

Suddenly, it was as if the world made sense again. I started to run, and no one could stop me. I took aim. The ball was flying through the air, and the keeper had no chance. He was standing with his mouth open watching the ball zoom over his head.

'Gooooaaaallllaaaa... Gooooaaaallllaaaa... Gooooaaaallllaaaa!'

I had won the Hope Games for the United Republic! I led the team up to the stage, and Reygo gave me a high five. And when I turned, I saw Il Presido holding the Cuppa, and he walked over to me. He saw I was a zombie, but he didn't care. He shook my hand and the crowd cheered.

I jumped awake, and my heart was beating hard, fast, and powerful. I leapt out of bed, energy pumping through my veins. I was standing in the dark, looking around with my red night vision. This was how I would see the whole world during the day if I fell into a dead zombie mist again. I pulled out the cold metal torch and switched it on. I turned the beam around the tent, over the heads of the other sleeping Awoken kids, and I saw everything in bright light. And that's when I remembered Dad, my brilliant dad! He was somewhere on the Mainland, hidden beyond my beam of light.

'*You work hard, and you try your best—that's why I'm proud of you every day.*'

I laughed for the first time in a long time because I was happy. Yes, it was only a dream, but what if it could come true? Nala was right—you must never give up. I knew now exactly what my purpose in life was. I couldn't wait for the next day.

23

NEW DREAMS

The next morning, nothing had changed but me. I was still stuck on the Island, but now I had hope and determination. I charged to find Nala and G-Nut in the mess. Nala was practicing her UFC routine with her stick.

'Good work, Nala! You're going to need those moves where we're going,' I told her. She smiled.

'Looks like Zanto's back,' she said.

'He sure is, and he's a zombie with a mission!' I said.

'Which is what?' Jack asked.

'First, I'm going to escape this stupid prison. Then I'm going to the Capital City where I'll infiltrate the United Republic soccer team. Then I'm going to score the winning goal in the final. Then I'll meet Il Presido, tell him what Capo Grey is doing here, and get all our friends released from the Island. And after that I'm going to find my dad!'

'Brilliant! Let's go!' Jack said.

'Okay...' Nala was more cautious. 'Obviously it's a great mission, but just how do we get off the Island?'

'Well, I do have an idea, only it's a bit risky.' I told them the plan.

'That sounds dangerous,' Nala said, her nose screwed up.

'Are you scared?' G-Nut teased her.

'Of course, I am,' she answered. 'Anyone with a brain would be.'

'I'm not!' G-Nut snorted.

'Exactly,' she said.

'So, are you in?' I asked them.

'Yeah let's escape!' G-Nut yelled.

'Shush, keep it down,' I warned.

Nala didn't answer for a bit, and then she smiled.

'I'm more scared of staying in this dump. Let's do it!' She grinned.

We all spat into our hands and shook.

* * * *

I shuffled off slowly to the hospital, making sure I still seemed hopeless and depressed. I found Dr Allen sitting behind her desk in her office. I knew what I was going to say was a huge risk, but we had no other options.

'I want you to help me get to the Mainland,' I said.

'Capo Grey will never allow it,' she replied.

'I mean an *escape*!' I said.

'Impossible,' she replied.

'But I have a plan. First, me, Nala and Jack act all DeeZee again. You say that we've changed back like Obi. The guards put us back in the Pen, and we get on the trucks for the Mainland.'

'But what if you're attacked in the Pen? Those un-awoken zombies treat you like humans now.'

The N-Deds never talked about us like we *were* human, only *like* humans!

'We'll use Agent Blue to disguise us,' I said.

'But that doesn't always work, and even if it did, it's still too dangerous,' she said. 'Those trucks are headed for the Iron City and it's overrun with man-eaters.'

'Really?' I hadn't expected that. 'But I thought the Iron City was just for the adults?'

'We've been ordered to send a hundred of our kid zombies there. I don't know why,' she said.

'Well, I'd rather take the risk than stay here.' I might have sounded tough, but now I was scared. 'Because if I stay here, my heart truly will give up, like Obi's. Then I'll go to the Pen for real.'

'Don't say that,' Dr Allen shook her head.

'It's true. I hate being in this cage. I want to live again. Please help us get on those trucks tonight, Doctor!'

It took her ages to answer, but at last, she nodded.

'Okay Zanto, I'll help you. Here, take this Agent Blue.' She handed me a bottle. 'Go back to your tent, and be ready. I'll do my inspection at six. But remember, you'll have to convince the guards you've fallen into the zombie sleep again.'

* * * *

My heart was beating fast with nerves. Nala had taken face paints from the play box. We dyed ourselves a brighter green than normal, and shaded red around our eyes. We sprayed ourselves with anti-zombie Agent Blue. Then it was time to play *dead*—or *heart broken*.

Jack lay on the bed next to mine, but Nala was in the girls' tent. I hoped that she got through okay, but I wouldn't know until we reached the Pen. I lay down, hands on my chest and closed my eyes, concentrating as hard as I could on slow breathing. I could hear Dr Allen approaching with her nurse and the two guards. This was it. The tent flap opened.

'Oh no. It looks like we've lost two more,' the nurse said.

'Let me check,' Dr Allen said. I peeped as she held Jack's wrist. 'This one's pulse has nearly stopped,' she lied. 'He's fallen back into the zombie sleep.'

'Careful ladies,' Grimm said. 'They could turn vicious if they...'

'Gnnarrragggh!' Jack leapt up, his eyes glaring and mouth screaming wide. He roared at them and made a swipe for the nurse who jumped back quick. I nearly jumped in surprise from my own *dead* sleep.

'He's turned. Hold him down,' Dr Allen said. 'I'll put him out.'

She took a needle filled with tranquiliser and injected him. Jack fell asleep.

I stayed completely still as they walked over to me. I felt Dr Allen take my wrist.

'Yes, this one has turned too,' she said. 'Best put him in the Pen with the others.'

'No, wait! Capo Grey won't allow that,' Flint said. 'Z51 is too valuable. We'll put him in an isolation cell here instead.'

Oh no, that would be a disaster!

'We can't break Capo Grey's rules,' Dr Allen said. 'Any awoken zombies who fall back into zombie sleep must go to the Pen.'

'But if anything happens to Z51, I'll have to answer for it,' Flint replied.

'What can happen to a *zombie* in a pen of zombies?' Dr Allen said. 'Capo Grey returns soon. If he's not happy, you can move Z51 into a cell then.'

'But are you sure he's actually a sleeping zombie again?' Flint asked. 'He doesn't look that sick. I'll check for myself.' I heard him step forward.

'Gnnarrragggh!' I hurled myself forward at Flint who yelped and jumped back. I knelt on the bed and snarled and raged at them, swiping my fingers if they tried to come near me.

'Crazy zombie scum!' The guard cried.

I screamed at him, and leapt off the bed, remembering how Romeo had run at me, arms swinging like a gorilla. Flint squealed and tripped over onto his backside.

'Don't let it bite me!' he cried.

'Exactly,' Dr Allen said, and injected me. I yelped as I felt the sharp needle sink into my backside. 'It's the Pen for you, my boy!' she said. And then her mouth came close to my ear. 'Good Luck, Zanto,' she whispered. 'Stay safe.'

I passed out.

24

BACK iN THE PEN

I was in the Pen, lying on my back on the dirt. I could hear the DeeZees all around me snuffling and snorting in the dark, but not screaming. In fact, they seemed very quiet. But what was scary was that I could *smell* them, and they reeked even worse than I remembered. I'd grown even less zombie and more like N-Ded since I'd last been in the Pen. They would surely smell me too and know I was different, and there were man-eaters in there.

I opened my eyes and saw red misty shapes in the night. I was surrounded by DeeZees standing and swaying in the dark, their arms and heads flopped down. I'd seen them do this before, through the fence—they were sleeping. I knelt up.

'Gnnarrragggh!'

A furious face, putrid green and spitting, was coming for me through the red mist. I was bowled over onto my back, fighting for my life. The zombie's dripping fangs were… were… were not so massive after all. I saw the carrot hair.

'G-Nut, you idiot!' I pushed him away angrily.

'Whoa, totally got you, Zero!' Jack bragged.

'Shut up, fool! We don't want to wake them up,' I hissed.

'Oh, lighten up, Zero. Since when you got so serious?'

'Don't you get it, Jack?' I whispered. 'Life's not a joke any more—it's precious and we have to fight for every moment of it now. And we're not just risking our own lives, but all our friends' lives too! We have one chance to get this right and save everyone. So, get your commando face on!'

'Hey man, it's on!' Jack grimaced.

'Have you seen Nala?'

'No. If we're lucky, she didn't make it.' Jack said.

'G-nut! Seriously? We make it together, or not at all. We need her, and she's as good a friend to you as me. So, grow up, and get over whatever problem you have with her. Come on, we need to find her before the trucks arrive at midnight.'

Using our zombie red night vision, we moved easily

through the dark, trying not to wake the DeeZees. It was pretty freaky though, zigzagging our way around them. The stench from their snores and farts made you want to gag. Still, we held our noses and kept walking. I gave a low whistle, the agreed signal to find each other, but there was still no sign of Nala.

We turned a corner and walked straight into a huge DeeZee with a ragged Mohican. His red eyes flashed open and glinted in the dark, and immediately he started snarling. He was clearly annoyed about being woken up.

'Oh-oh, this ain't good,' Ginga-Nut said. I agreed with him.

'Let's hope the Agent Blue works.'

The DeeZee opened its mouth and screamed at us so loud it was like a toxic wind blasting us. Bits of rotting flesh dangling from its face shook. I nearly passed out.

The noise woke up the DeeZees behind us and they all started to screech too. I did the only thing I could think of and screamed back at them. Jack did too. We stood there back to back, screaming at the crowd of furious zombies that were encircling us. Mohican DeeZee started to move towards us, its jaws hammering together like it meant business. The Agent Blue wasn't working with him.

'We have to go quickly!' I said and grabbed Jack's arm.

I pushed a couple of little DeeZees aside. We barged through the circle, shrugging off the grabbing talons and ran to where some zombies were still asleep. But, the ones we left behind started screeching at full volume. As we ran, a Mexican wave of zombie heads lifted up as they sprang into furious life and followed us. Then the wave overtook us, and we saw the DeeZees ahead wake up too. We skidded to a halt next to a stone hut. We were trapped.

'Why isn't the Agent Blue working?' G-nut hissed.

'Perhaps because of our zombie mutation?'

'What do we do now?' G-Nut asked, out of breath.

'Hope that they're vegetarians,' I said.

'That one's not,' G-Nut pointed at a DeeZee.

'Gnnarrragggh.' A huge green DeeZee lurched towards us. There was nowhere to run. The others behind us were screaming too.

Pah-pah-thonk!

A figure jumped in front of us and whacked the legs from under the charging zombie with a big stick. The DeeZee's speed made it crash into the wall, and it passed out. All the other zombies stopped roaring, like they were waiting to see what happened next.

'Need a rescue, boys?' Nala asked.

I laughed to see her.

'Not sure it's a rescue yet,' I said, as the whole DeeZee hoard began to surround us.

'Looks like we'll die fighting,' G-Nut said.

'Guess so,' Nala swung her stick once more.

We stood with our backs to the wall, facing the hoard, Nala with her stick, and Jack and I with our fists and karate kicks ready. We could see fangs glinting in the red mist of the dark. They were definitely some man-eaters. I turned on my torch and shone it in their eyes. They screamed and turned away. Only as soon as I flashed it at other DeeZees, they stepped forward again. In the bright light, we could see their rotting skin and putrid yellow boils better than with our zombie night vision.

Nala whacked an attacking DeeZee on its head with her stick and it roared with outrage. The circle was getting tighter. I karate kicked one, and G-Nut punched another. They moved closer still.

There was one very mean-looking zombie with white-blonde hair. It reminded me of GN1, but it wasn't him. This gangster-looking DeeZee threw itself at Nala, clearly wanting to eat her. I kicked it as hard as I'd ever kicked a football and it fell down. But another immediately took its place. We couldn't hold them back much longer.

'We're dead!' G-Nut yelled.

'I'm not dying here, no way!' Nala said, as she whacked a girl DeeZee and knocked it unconscious. 'Come on boys, we can do it. Just imagine what you're going to be in ten years. I'll be a doctor. I'm going to fight to stay alive.' She whacked another DeeZee. 'I'm going to live my dream!'

'Yeah right!' I cried and kicked another one back. 'I'm going to score that goal and save these kids, even if they want to eat me!'

'You're fooling yourselves, we're all goners!' Jack said, as the zombies charged.

25

IN DANGER

Whoosh!

A huge jet of water gushed across the yard. It knocked the legs out from under the charging zombies and washed them away. Big overhead spotlights flashed on and lit up the whole Pen. I peeped around the stone hut and saw the guards there with a water cannon mounted on a truck. The DeeZees were in a heaving tangled muddle of bodies and limbs. They roared with outrage and tried to stand up again, but another blast from the canon pushed them even further away. Then we heard the low rumble.

'The trucks are coming,' I said. 'Get ready.'

'We'd planned to get on the trucks when we thought Agent Blue would work,' Jack said. 'But we won't be safe in there now with that lot!' He pointed at the DeeZees.

'Well, we can't stay here,' Nala replied.

'This was your stupid plan, Captain Zero,' G-Nut hissed at me. 'Who put a *retard* in charge?'

'Oi! Leave Zanto alone!' Nala cried. 'He's trying to save all the Awoken!'

'If we'd stayed in the hospital, at least *we'd* be alive,' Jack insisted.

'No, we wouldn't, Jack,' I said. 'One by one, we would have fallen into the zombie sleep again, like Obi. We had to run. I never want to be a DeeZee again.'

'And I don't want to be eaten in chunks!' Jack replied.

'No one made you come,' Nala said to him. 'Stop moaning and find a backbone!'

I put my hand on Jack's shoulder.

'I know you're scared, mate, so am I. But the only way out now is in one of those trucks.'

The gates swung open and three big trucks drove in, turned, and stopped with their rears towards us. Soldiers jumped out, holding laser guns. They dropped the tailgates of the trucks to form ramps, then waited for the tangle of wet zombies to stand up. The DeeZees staggered to their feet, snarling and screaming at the soldiers. They'd forgotten about us three completely. Perhaps they'd smelled something much tastier. As they walked forward, the soldiers began to herd them, exactly as we'd seen before, by shining bright beams at them.

'You ready?' I asked Nala and took her hand.

'Ready,' she nodded. 'But I feel a bit sick.'

'Me too,' I admitted. 'You coming, G-Nut?' I asked him. Jack glared at me but nodded. 'Remember to act like a DeeZee!' I warned.

We staggered forward, Nala trailing her pole behind her. We snarled and glared at the soldiers as we slouched past. I saw the gangster man-eater who'd tried to attack Nala nearby, only now he didn't even glance our way, too busy trying to reach the soldiers.

We'd almost reached the trucks, and the crowd was getting tight. Zombies were staggering up ramps and the trucks were filling faster than I'd expected. I started to worry we wouldn't make it on.

'Push forward. Don't get separated,' I whispered, without moving my lips.

'Stop!' Flint yelled.

My heart jumped hard. I dropped my head and started snarling, just as furious as any DeeZee could be.

'That zombie is Z51. You can't take it, it's too valuable. Capo Grey will want to keep it,' he said.

My head shrank with fright. I tried to push faster. Nala gripped on tightly.

'This operation is under Army command, not Capo Grey's,' the soldier replied. 'And we're not risking any men going into that rabid mob for a pet zombie.'

We'd reached the ramp. I could see Jack shuffling up ahead of me. I could hear Flint still arguing, but lucky for us, the officer wouldn't listen.

'That's it, we're full!' a soldier cried.

They threw a rope across the zombie crowd to stop them. I made it past, but Nala was on the wrong side. I saw panic in her eyes. The soldiers began to pull on the rope, yanking the DeeZees back.

'Duck down, quick!' I whispered and raised the rope.

I pulled her forward with me onto the truck.

'Look, it's still alive!' Flint shouted. 'We've been tricked. It's escaping. Stop, Z51!'

The doors slammed shut and plunged us into red-black vision.

'You two okay?' I whispered.

'Yeah!'

'For now...'

Jack and Nala sounded as scared as I felt. We knew we weren't any safer inside that truck. We huddled together at the back. The noise of zombies screeching, and the stench of their rotting flesh was horrendous. We'd escaped the Pen; but now we were trapped in a truck with the DeeZees.

The engine started. I expected Flint to yank open the doors and pull me back at any moment. Inside the truck, the DeeZees were furious they'd been locked in. They were banging on the sides and the front, trying to get out. Their talons were scraping down the metal so that it hurt your ears. Perhaps they could still smell the soldiers and wanted to reach them.

The truck moved forward. The zombies all lurched and some fell, as they couldn't balance as well as we could. There was a gap in the metal panel doors and I looked out. We were leaving the Pen. I saw the gates close behind us and Flint glaring as the trucks left. As scared as I was, that made me smile.

'We're out!' I whispered to Nala and Jack.

I watched as the lights of the Pen disappeared into the night, then I turned around.

The zombies were all still busy banging on the doors and the front of the cab. Thankfully, they seemed to be ignoring us three at the back. Now and then, a DeeZee nearby would turn to us and screech in our faces, and we would screech back. But that's when I saw him again: the gangster DeeZee with white hair. He was sniffing the air. Suddenly, he turned his head towards us and roared. He began trying to push his way through the sprawling crowd to reach us.

'Get ready, he's going to attack,' I warned the others. There was a large spanner on a hook on the back of the door. I grabbed it.

'Here,' I handed my torch to G-Nut. Nala had her stick ready.

We watched as the gangster struggled to get through. He was getting closer. The truck turned a sharp bend, and all the zombies fell into a pile of squirming bodies and limbs. There was a tiny little kid DeeZee under the pile getting squashed. I reached over, pulled her up, and put her back on her feet. She hissed at me and tried to swipe me with her talons.

'It's a pleasure,' I told her and turned her round to face the other way.

The white-haired zombie stood up, and lurched towards us. Jack shone the torch in his eyes, and he shrieked and turned away. That only attracted a growl from the other side of the truck. The Mohican man-eater was there too! Jack turned the torch to him, but that meant Gangster could come forward again. They were closing in on us. And then, when I thought things couldn't get any worse, they did!

Through the red mist of our night vision, we saw a huge figure rise up in front of us. He was a DeeZee full of ripped muscle, with his back to us. He could tear us apart. He turned and screamed in our faces, and my heart nearly broke because it was Obi! His once kind brown eyes were red and seething. Jack shone the light at him, and he roared with fury and smashed our torch onto the floor. Nala tried to use her pole, but he snatched it from her. I raised my spanner, but he bashed it away. It clanked off the head of a dopey-looking zombie and bounced back at us.

'Gnnarrragggh!' Obi roared.

We cowered into the corner. Behind Obi, the two man-eaters, Gangster and Mohican, had reached us. That was the moment I knew I was going to die again. Gangster tried to swipe Nala, but Obi hurled him backwards into the truck.

'Gnnarrragggh!' he roared at them.

The Mohican's talons were gripping Jack's sleeve. Obi snarled again and threw him backwards too. Then he turned to us, his yellow fangs dripping.

But Obi didn't attack us. No, he stayed in front of us, snarling and screeching at all the others. Nala reached forward and put her hand on his shoulder.

'Are you mad?' G-Nut cried. 'Don't make him angrier.'

Obi turned around, looked at Nala, and didn't roar. Instead, he stared at her, fascinated. Nala looked back at his red eyes and said his name. Obi bent his head to one side, like he was trying to understand. Nala moved her hand to his chest, and still he didn't attack her.

'I can feel his heart beating,' she said. 'He's still in there.'

'He can't be,' G-Nut said. And I was too scared to hope for it too.

'He is. He remembers us, he's protecting us!' Nala cried and threw her arms around him. I held my breath, waiting for him to attack her, but he didn't.

'Gnnarrrag-Gnnarrral,' he snarled, then shook his head. 'Nnarrr-laaaaa,' he growled.

'He's saying your name!' I cried. 'He's still alive!'

I hugged him too, and his body was warm. Somehow, Obi's broken heart had mended—maybe it was because he'd left the Pen. Even inside his dark zombie mist, he'd found some hope again. He pushed us off and roared, because the man-eaters weren't giving up that easily.

What followed was the best fight I've ever seen. DeeZee kids were flying everywhere, and then crawling back for more, but no one could take Obi down—he was like some sort of green superman. At the end, it seemed even the DeeZees had learned their lesson, because for rest of the journey they gave up and left us alone. They slumped in a zombie stupor, exhausted. While they slept, I found my torch and kept it safe.

We owed Obi our lives. Without him, we'd never have got off that Island except as chunks in zombie stomachs.

26

ESCAPE FROM THE ISLAND

We heard seagulls as we approached the harbour. Our trucks drove straight onto a ferry, and I felt the sea rocking the boat. The soldier-drivers jumped out, and their boots clattered on the metal floor as they walked away. Some of the man-eaters in the truck began to growl and look like they were peckish enough for a fight again. Obi snarled at them and they stayed put.

'Okay, time for the next part of the plan,' I said. This was Nala's idea.

We rubbed the bright green paint off our faces, necks, and arms. Then, we unloaded the dress-up paints and crayons we'd stashed in our pockets before we'd been put into the Pen. Obi watched, his head to one side, as Nala painted Ginga-Nut with pale pink flesh-coloured paint. She used brown eye shadow to cover his red eyelids. She painted his black nails pale pink.

'Very pretty,' I laughed as she put lipstick on him.

Jack glared at me. 'Kiss my backside!'

'No, thanks.'

When Nala had finished, Jack didn't look 100% like his old self, but he did look vaguely N-Ded. Nala painted me the same colour as Jack. It wasn't as good a match for me, because I used to be tanned, and now I was way too pale. But it was a better disguise for the Mainland than being green.

'I'm starting to think this plan might work,' Jack said looking at me.

'Me too,' I said, 'if only we can open this door before we get to the Iron City.'

Jack picked up the spanner and started looking at the door. There was a long steel rod with bolts, which were the workings for the lock on the inside of the truck.

'I think I've got an idea,' he said. He was always good at building or destroying stuff.

While Jack inspected the door, I painted Nala's face with a dark brown flesh colour that seemed to match how I remembered her when she was first alive. I put the brown eye shadow on Nala's red eyelids, and then the lipstick. It was nice to see her looking like old Nala. I guess she even looked a bit pretty, for a girl.

'Okay then, Obi, it's your turn...'

I moved to put the brown paint on Obi's face, only he growled at me. I stepped back. He was still more DeeZee than living human.

'Let me try,' Nala said. 'See?' She showed the make-up to him. 'It won't hurt you.'

She reached up and dabbed his face with brown paint, and he didn't pull away. He had a few yellow boils that needed covering up, but no rotten flesh.

I watched, fascinated, as he was transformed back into something like he must have looked before he first died. He could have been Nala's big brother.

'Your nails, Obi,' Nala pointed. 'Too big! Do you understand? Bite them off...' She did a demo.

Obi bit his talons until they looked like normal nails. Then Nala painted them pink. Obi inspected them, and he smiled, showing his not so beautiful massive yellow fangs.

'Don't smile,' Nala shook her head. 'Stay like this!' She clamped her mouth shut and pointed at it. Obi closed his mouth tight.

'Yes. Well done,' Nala smiled.

He smiled back, then remembered, and clamped his mouth shut again.

'Watch out!' I shouted.

One of the man-eaters was sneaking up behind Nala. Obi stood up and roared. Even with new N-Ded coloured skin, he was a pretty terrifying zombie, and his eyeballs were still furious red. The man-eater scampered backwards quickly.

'We need to get him some sunglasses,' I said.

'I can open the door,' Jack said. 'See, if we loosen these two bolts here...' He showed us. It wasn't a complicated system.

'Then let's go now, before the soldiers come back,' I said. 'They might not stop on the Mainland until they reach Iron City. Agreed?'

'Agreed!' Nala and Jack said.

'Aaagnreer,' said Obi.

I held the torch for Jack, and he began to loosen the two bolts. It made a terrible metallic screeching noise that got the DeeZees really worked up. They started to stand up and hiss. Obi snarled back at them, but they looked ready for another fight.

'Better hurry,' I said to Jack.

'I am,' he replied and kept on loosening the bolts.

One of the man-eaters made a charge at Obi, but he pushed it back.

'Faaassssstttt,' he said. He was remembering how to talk.

By now, all the zombies were crawling forward. I shone my torch at the nearest ones, and they screeched and moved back.

'I need the light, Zero,' Jack said. He was struggling with the second bolt. I shone it back to him.

Thwack.

Nala kicked a DeeZee and it fell backwards.

'Hurry,' she said.

'I *am!*' Jack replied.

The zombies surged forwards.

'It's done—go!' Jack yelled.

The door swung open, and we three jumped out onto the metal floor of the ferry. We were on a covered vehicle deck, and no one was around. Obi was still in the truck, throwing the DeeZees back. He grappled with the gangster man-eater.

'Obi, you have to come now!' Nala called to him.

Obi hurled the zombie away and leapt out of the truck. We tried to push the door closed. But, the DeeZees were trying to jump out after us, and we couldn't lock it. Obi took a run up and hurled himself at the door. It slammed shut and Jack locked the bolt. The DeeZees trapped inside roared with fury.

'We did it!' Nala hugged me.

Obi stared to laugh—a strange growling noise—then he clamped his mouth shut to hide his fangs.

'What now?' Jack asked.

'We find somewhere to hide till we reach the Mainland,' I said.

There was staircase next to us, but we reckoned that was too dangerous. Instead, we walked towards an exit, near the back of the deck. As we passed a car, I saw the driver had left his sunglasses inside. I tried the door—it was open. I knew Dad wouldn't approve of stealing, but this was an emergency. I opened the door and took out the sunglasses—they were mirror Aviators. I handed them to Obi. He put them on and then admired himself from several angles in the wing mirror. He nodded, very pleased with himself. He did look cool.

There was a door with "*Crew Only*" written on it. We piled through and found a narrow set of stairs going up. At the top, we opened the door, escaped onto the open deck, and bumped into a man and woman. I expected them to scream because we were zombies, but they just smiled and nodded. They thought we were normal kids! This was going to work. We smiled back—well, Obi didn't. But then I saw they were screwing their noses up and wafting the air away. We smelled different, and OBI still smelled dead. Still they didn't seem to make the connection and walked away.

We were on an open deck. The wind was blowing, and the night sky was full of stars. We weren't safe yet, but already I felt free. I leaned over the rail and saw the black sea below us, swelling and heaving. At last, we were out of prison and off the Island. We could dare to hope for real lives again, in which we were allowed to have names and dreams, and perhaps even a new home.

Then I had a reality check. The people who'd seen us only treated us like normal because we'd painted over our green skin. How would they react if they knew we were actually *zombies*? Would they give us a chance to explain we were Awoken? Or like Capo Grey predicted, would they attack us before we could hurt them?

'How about we hide in here?' Nala said, lifting the canvas on a lifeboat.

We climbed inside and pulled the cover back over. Despite the fact it was uncomfortable and cramped, I had the best sleep that I could remember having since turning into a zombie.

27

THE MAINLAND

I could hear seagulls, and I was freezing cold. I peeped from under the canvas. It was a grey cloudy morning, and we'd docked at the Mainland. It was time to finish our escape. But I saw that Obi had a bit of green showing on his face, so we all touched up our make-up again.

'Don't you think you've got enough on now?' I asked Jack, as he caked extra lipstick on.

'No,' he squinted into a bit of polished metal. 'Just a bit more, so I look N-Ded.'

I said he looked like an N-Ded with too much lipstick on. Obi broke into a big fang-filled grin. We reminded him not to smile and climbed out of the lifeboat.

From the deck, we watched the soldiers drive off the ferry with the three trucks. They hadn't noticed that we'd gone. But I felt bad for the DeeZee kids being sent to the Iron City. Mutated man-eating zombies had overrun the whole place. I hoped they'd be okay. There were some foot passengers departing down the metal ramp.

'We'd better go with them,' Nala said.

We tried to loiter behind, so as not to be noticed. The other passengers ignored us until we walked past an old sailor with a beard who looked like Captain Birdseye. He stared at us. Then he frowned and walked over.

'Just act normal,' I whispered to the others.

'I am normal,' Jack said under his breath—big words for a zombie with rouge and lipstick on. But, the old sailor just waved us off. I was relieved to get off the boat without any questions. We walked towards the harbour exit.

'So, what now?' Nala asked.

'First, we go to the Capital City,' I said. 'Find '*Ye Old Candy Shoppe*' in the East Quarter, like Jack's mum told us. She said her friends would help us. Then I'll need to find the soccer team and infiltrate it.'

I could see Obi was listening intently.

'Jack's mum's friends were going to help us when we were humans,' Nala said. 'They may not be so keen on zombies turning up. They might hand us over to the police. And *they'll* send us back to the Island, or worse, the Iron City.' She was right.

'If you've got another plan, we can try that,' I said. 'I

don't know what else to do.'

'No, I don't have any other ideas,' she shrugged.

'I'm going to the Candy Shoppe,' Jack said. 'Ma might be there'.

'Caaannnddddy Shhoopppe,' Obi growled in agreement.

'So, how do we get to the Capital City?' I wondered.

'What about that?' Jack pointed.

A truck was driving off the ferry. It had tall sides, but the top was open, only covered by a few metal slats. On the side was written:

'*Farm Fresh—Best produce from the Island to The Capital every morning.*'

'Good work G-Nut,' I high-fived him.

'I know.' he nodded.

The truck began to drive slowly past us and towards the harbour exit. We weren't going to get another chance like this.

'Let's go—quick!' I cried.

We started running. I reached the back of the truck first. There was a narrow step along the bottom of it that I jumped onto. Obi got on next. Nala and Jack were running side-by-side, only Jack stumbled a bit. Nala turned to check if he was okay and didn't see a pothole. She staggered sideways, as Jack sped up again.

'Help her!' I yelled to him. But perhaps he didn't hear, because he kept running and jumped onto the back with us. Nala was running as fast as she could, I could see her face in pain, like she had a stitch. The truck was speeding up.

'Faster!' I called to her.

She was almost there, but I didn't think she could do it. I got ready to jump back off again.

'Noooo,' Obi stopped me. He held onto the back of the truck, leaned right out behind, and put out his other hand to Nala.

'Come on!' I yelled. It was her last chance.

She reached out, and Obi grabbed her wrist. He lifted her high and swung her onto the back step with us like she didn't weigh anything. Nala couldn't speak for a while, only hold onto the truck until she caught her breath again.

'Thanks,' she managed at last.

'OOOOOO Kaaayyy,' Obi grinned, his sharp yellow fangs flashing.

We climbed up and dropped down inside onto the bags of potatoes and cabbages.

* * * *

A few hours later, the clouds lifted, and the sun came out at last. It was late afternoon. We were approaching the Capital City. None of us had ever been there before. We climbed the sides of the truck and peeped out to see ahead.

'Whoa!' G-Nut said—and I agreed.

It was nothing like the Iron City, which was all smoking industrial factories and drab grey concrete office blocks. The Capital seemed to be all beautiful tall buildings made from shining steel, mirrors, and glass, all reflecting back the sun. I didn't know such places existed.

We drove past enormous department stores with windows as big as our old house. The displays of beautiful things you could buy were like scenes from a magical story. The people walking down the street all looked rich and perfect, dressed in expensive clothes. No wonder they would rather bomb the Shambles than allow their beautiful city to be overrun by zombies.

Perhaps my dad was still somewhere here. Only I couldn't imagine him walking down these streets in his work gear, nor even dressed in his church Sunday best jacket and trousers. He just didn't look like these people.

The truck took a turn and drove into a side street. It had to stop at some traffic lights. There was no one around.

'Reckon we should get out here,' Jack said.

'Good idea,' Nala agreed.

We climbed out of the truck and dropped onto the road before it took off again.

'So far so easy,' I said.

'Zanto, come here,' Nala said.

'What?' I turned to her.

'I see some green showing,' she said, and painted more make-up on my cheek. 'That's better. The last thing we want is anyone guessing we're zombies.'

'Too right! They'll attack us for sure. They won't wait to ask questions.' Jack said. 'We must never show what we truly are.'

I felt sick with nerves. Because I knew that if I wanted to change people's minds, convince them zombies weren't all dangerous, and help free the Awoken, then at some point I'd have to do exactly that. I'd have to show them my green skin, show them I was one of the zombies they were terrified of, and hope they didn't neutralise me.

I hadn't told the others that part of my plan. But I wondered if Nala had guessed. The way she was looking at me made me think she knew what I was thinking.

'Keeepp moooviiing,' Obi said.

Two men suddenly appeared ahead of us. We were nervous to pass them. Surely, they'd see there was something strange about our skin. Only they walked right past us and didn't even glance our way. Feeling more confident, we walked on. It was the same in the main streets—nobody took any notice of anyone else. Everyone was focused on their own business. We felt braver every second.

I stopped in the street for a moment, feeling blown away by it all. The people all walked around me like I was a stone in a stream and they were the racing water. I was a zombie kid in the Capital, free at last, and no one seemed bothered by it.

'Come on, Zanto, we need to find shelter,' Nala said and pointed at more clouds gathering to the east. 'What if it rains? Do you think they'd still ignore us when we're green?' She was right.

We kept walking east. There was a huge crowd going the same way and all dressed in football colours.

'Where are you all going?' Nala asked a girl.

'The Hope Games, of course. It's the Boys' Football Final—The United Republic against West Kingdom.'

'The final's today?' I cried in concern. 'Then I have to get to the Crystal Stadium. That's where Il Presido will be. I saw it in my dream. I'm going to score a goal and meet him. That's when I'll tell him about the Island.'

'No, we're going to the Candy Shoppe, like we agreed,' Jack said. 'That's what Ma said.'

'G-Nut, I have to play in that match—it's my destiny! The future of all the Awoken depends on it,' I told him.

'You don't really believe that, do you?' Jack laughed. 'It's just a stupid fantasy. We have to save ourselves.'

'But you agreed to the plan!' I reminded him.

'Yeah, to get off the Island and get here.' Jack said. 'But the rest of it is just some mad dream of yours. You're not going to play in the final, Zero. Zack Starr has already picked his team, and you're not in it! And you won't meet Reygo, or Il Presido.'

'But I have to play. I have to score the goal. It's the only way I can save the other kids.'

'Wake up, dude. You're not saving anyone, because you're not a hero. You're just a Zero, a *zombie*!' G-Nut continued. 'And if you tell anyone that, you'll end up in the Iron City, or neutralised.'

Perhaps he was right, but what else could I do? Give up? No way!

'I have to risk it,' I said.

'It's your funeral, man, seriously! I'm going to the Candy Shoppe where mum's friends will hide me.'

'We've got to stick together, Jack,' Nala warned.

'Yeah, we do. So, are you guys coming or not?' he replied.

'I go where Zanto goes,' Nala said.

'Meee tooo,' said Obi.

'Whatever, losers,' G-Nut said and stormed off. 'Send me a post card from the Iron City.'

I was sorry to see him go, but I knew what I had to do.

28

THE CRYSTAL STADIUM

I'd always dreamed of seeing the Gladiatorum, Real Magique's ground, but as I looked over the heads of the crowd and saw the Crystal Stadium ahead, I thought this was almost as good. It was as beautiful as it sounded, shining like pink gems in the dying sunset, a tower on each corner with our national flag waving in the breeze. Inside the stadium, the massive floodlights were already on. Everyone around was buzzing with excitement. Hanging on the wall was a huge picture of Zack Starr—'*Our Captain and National Hero.*'

'I can't stand that guy,' Nala said.

She'd never forgive him for what he'd said about us. But I didn't care too much that Zack Starr was the captain, because my heart was beating fast and I felt alive. I imagined the teams inside: the two best boy soccer teams in the world, waiting to play in the final. It must be the best feeling in the world.

Suddenly, I felt cold and the stadium stopped shining. The sun had gone down and black clouds were gathering in the dusk sky. Still I wouldn't let that dampen my hopes. I didn't know how I was going to get on that pitch, but even if I had to jump down from the crowd, I was going to do it. This was my destiny, I just knew it. We'd almost reached the turnstiles.

'Probbbbb...lem,' Obi said, without opening his mouth too much. 'No tickkk-ets and no monnnn-ey.' He was almost talking normally again.

Fireworks went off overhead as the final started. We did a complete circle of the stadium, but it was no use: there was no way in without a ticket. None of the guards would let us in. I didn't want to give up, but what else could we do? I sat down on the ground in frustration. It was almost dark, and my red night vision was kicking in. I couldn't believe my dream would end like this, stuck on the outside of the stadium. We heard a huge roar.

'A goooaaal,' Obi said.

The game was going on and would finish without me. My dream hadn't been a premonition, just a fantasy, like Jack said. I wasn't going to play, wasn't going to score, and wasn't going to save anyone. I felt a few drops of water on me.

'Raaain!' Obi said. 'Baaaad.'

He was right—it would be a disaster, as our flesh co-loured paint would wash off.

'Zanto, we have to go quick and hide somewhere,' Nala said. 'I'm so sorry, but we can't stay here. You tried your best, but we have to stay safe too.'

'Yeah, I know, okay.' I forced my body to find some energy. 'Let's go to the Old Candy Shoppe then.'

But then I heard a dreadful screeching noise behind us. A metal door marked '*Staff Only*' was opening. An old man came out with some rubbish bags that he threw into a large bin.

'Hi kids,' he said. 'The game's already started. West Kingdom is up one nil—you'd better get inside. The turn-styles are that way,' he pointed. He looked kind and reminded me of my dad.

'We can't afford tickets,' I told him. 'We're too poor. Can you let us in, please? We so want to see Reygo.'

The old man frowned.

'I can't let anyone in here. I could lose my job.'

I sagged once more.

'Oh well then, who'll ever know?' the old man whispered. 'Come on in quick, kids!'

My head shot up and my heart felt like it was beating fast again. We ran to the door.

'They worry about security, but what harm can this do?' The old man said. 'It's not like I'm letting in three zombies, is it?' He threw his head back and gave a big laugh.

'Zombies, us?' I roared. 'What a joke.'

'As if!' Nala agreed, with big snort.

'Gnar-gnar-gnar,' Obi laughed too, his massive yellow fangs revealed for all to see. I reached up and clamped my hand over his mouth quick, but the old man was too busy closing the door again to notice. We thanked him and ran down the corridor.

We were somewhere underneath the building. We could hear the roar of the crowds above.

'What's your plan now, Zanto?' Nala asked me.

'I've no idea. All I know is I have to score a goal, and that way I can talk to Il Presido.'

'Okay,' she said. 'But how do we get you on the pitch?'

'Something will happen,' I said. 'I know it will.'

There was another huge roar.

'Gooooal!' Obi said.

We turned a corner, and my heart beat even faster in excitement because I could see light.

'Look,' I whispered. 'It's the players' tunnel!'

We crept up the slope towards the light. As we moved, the noise from the crowd got louder, like a wave growing. There were some security guys at the top of the tunnel, standing a couple of metres onto the ground. They were too busy watching the game to look behind them. We reached the edge of the tunnel, and I looked up at the inside of the stadium.

It was amazing. A huge bowl surrounded by the cheering crowd. The pitch was lit by massive floodlights. The people were going wild: roaring, waving flags, and doing the Mexican Wave. I saw the scoreboard. West Kingdom 2—United Republic 0, with thirty minutes played. That meant fifteen minutes until half time.

We watched United Republic play, and I could see that they had no belief, and no hope of coming back. Their heads were down, and they never came close to scoring. Zack Starr was wearing the 7 shirt, and the best player by far was our number 9, a kid called Billy Pace. But even when Billy was in a good scoring position, Zack wouldn't pass him the ball. Zack was a good player, but the worst captain I'd ever seen.

He was either fouling the opposition, or else pushing and yelling at his own team. He never praised or encouraged them. When he did get the ball, he showed off with fancy footwork when he should have been driving forward. Or else, he passed badly and then yelled at *another* poor kid because he couldn't clean up Zack's mistake.

Zack fouled again, a nasty kick on the West Kingdom forward's shins.

'He'll get sent off if he's not careful,' Obi said, and he sounded totally like old Obi again. He took his sunglasses off and his pupils were black, not red.

'You're completely back again!' Nala gave him a hug.

'Yeah, I feel back,' he said, and it didn't sound like a growl.

'But you've still got massive yellow fangs,' I told him.

'I'll be careful,' he said. 'Now Zanto, we have to get you on that field somehow. I believe in you, mate. You can win this game. And then, when you meet Il Presido, that'll be the time to show them what you truly are!'

'You knew that I planned to show my green skin to everyone in the stadium?' I asked.

'Of course we knew, Zanto.' Nala smiled. 'And we'll be standing next to you showing our skin too.'

'But it's dangerous,' I said.

'We'll take that risk,' Obi shrugged. 'But we're never going back to that Pen. All in together!' He held his fist out, and we all touched fists.

West Kingdom nearly scored three more times. It was only because of the United Republic's brilliant goalkeeper that we were still in the game. Our coach was going mad on the sidelines, yelling at the boys to get forward. But they couldn't, or didn't know how to. They didn't have a leader for a captain, just a selfish show-off, full-of-himself.

The half-time whistle blew. We snuck back down the tunnel, hid in a side door, and watched the two teams walk down to their changing rooms. West Kingdom's players were pumped up and chatting. The United Republic boys were quiet, heads down, and dragging their tired legs. They reminded me of the DeeZees, the same hopelessness! Zack Starr came down last, furious. He was holding a towel and arguing with his coach.

'They're all useless!' he yelled. 'I can't win the game on my own.' He was shrieking like a spoiled child.

'You need to more careful with your passing, Zack,' the coach said. 'And stop bullying the other boys; it doesn't help.'

'I'm the only good player!' Zack shrieked even louder. 'If we lose, it's your fault.'

'Perhaps it is—for letting you be captain!' the coach yelled back. 'I know you left out any players you thought were better than you, you nasty little worm.'

Zack Starr hurled his towel down and stamped on it.

'My uncle will fire you and have you arrested!' he yelled. 'He's Il Presido—he'll do whatever I ask him to.'

'So, sack me,' the coach said and kept walking. 'Or else come in for the team talk.'

'No! I know how to play—it's the others you need to talk to.'

'You better be ready with a new attitude when that whistle blows, or I'll replace you with Fritz Best.'

The coach disappeared into the changing room, and Zack Starr stayed where he was, his arms crossed, sulking.

'I can't stand that kid,' Obi said and gave me a wink. 'This is your way in, Zanto.'

He ran forward, picked up the towel, and wrapped it round Zack's head. He threw the boy over his shoulder and charged off down a dark corridor. We could just hear Zack's muffled cries. Nala and I raced off after them.

Zack was sitting on the concrete floor, with Obi standing over him, his big arms folded. We were next to a storeroom door; and outside it were three huge plastic bins. Nala picked up a broom and kicked off the head, so that she had her favourite weapon again. She swung it, feeling the balance.

'You can't kidnap me!' Zack said. 'You're in trouble now.'

'No, son, you're the one in trouble,' Obi bared his fangs in a growl. Then he raised his shirt and showed Zack his green stomach. Zack shuffled back in fright, his eyes wide.

'You're a zombie!'

'We're all zombies, son.'

We smiled and nodded as Zack gaped at us.

Nala twirled the pole around her head, then made an ultimate warrior pounce, her stick pointed at Zack's head.

'Are you going to…eat me?' Zack stammered.

'Not *right this minute*. But I can't promise I won't get peckish later,' Obi said. Zack didn't look too relieved.

'What I need now,' Obi went on, 'is your kit and boots.'

'Why?' Zack looked suspicious.

'It's a matter of life and death.' Obi said.

'And because our team needs a real captain,' said Nala.

'Like who?' Zack glared.

'Surely you recognise Zanto here?' Obi said. 'Last time you saw him, you said he wasn't good enough for your team because he was green.'

Zack looked at me hard, then screwed his face up.

'You're the zombie from the Island?' he cried.

'That's right,' I said.

'You can't be captain. It's *my* team, and I'm the best player in it.'

'No, you're not,' I said. 'Billy Pace is better than you. And our team is trailing, and you don't know how to inspire them.'

'That's not true, I'm the best player in the whole Republic!' he yelled.

'No, you're not,' I said. 'I am. And I'm going out there to prove it.'

'But you're a zombie!' he shrieked. 'You smell like death!'

'Just hand over your number 7 shirt; you don't deserve it,' Nala said.

'If you go on that pitch, the team won't follow you. They'll see you for the scum you are. And the army will neutralise you, for good.'

'I'll risk it,' I said.

'You'll all pay for this!' He glared at us.

'Probably, son. But we're going to do it anyway.' Obi said.

29

THE IMPOSTER

'Zack. Where are you? The whistle's about to blow,' I heard the coach call from the top of the tunnel. 'You need to lead this team.'

Zack gave a muffled cry from inside the plastic bin that Obi had put him in.

'Yeah, I'm coming!' I yelled.

This was it then—my moment had arrived. I was dressed in a perfect red kit, with number 7 on my back, as close to being Reygo as I was ever going to be. I was ready to fulfil my destiny and save the Awoken. Perhaps this was why I'd been so good at football—everything had led to this moment.

But it was then we heard the noise from inside the storeroom behind us, unmistakable growls. I looked at the others.

'Sounds like DeeZees,' I said.

Nala looked a bit alarmed, but Obi shook his head.

'How can it be? We're in the Capital City. There are no zombies here,' he said.

'*We're* here,' I reminded him.

'You just go and show then what you can do, Zanto. Score goals. That's your job,' Obi smiled. 'Leave security to me.'

'Yeah, go on, Zanto,' Nala said. 'Win the final, meet Il Presido, and tell him about the Awoken. All in together!' We all touched fists again.

I ran up the tunnel towards the floodlit pitch. This was it. I was actually going to step out into the Crystal Stadium. The two teams were out on the pitch already. They were waiting for the captain on the centre circle. I looked up at the black sky, worried that it might still be raining, but the shower had passed. I saw our coach to my right, signalling frantically for me (Zack) to get in position. I recognised the kid standing next to him. It was Fritz Best. Like Zack, he looked vaguely like me from a distance, skinny with black hair. I needed his name.

I saw the fourth referee on the sidelines and ran up to him.

'Hi. I'm Fritz Best,' I told him. 'Coach has substituted me for Zack Starr.'

'Okay,' he said and noted it down with his pen. 'But get a move on. We need to start the game.'

I'd used Zack's kit and Fritz's name to sneak on, but my cover wouldn't survive an inspection, nor the close-ups on the giant TV screens above the crowd. Still, I'd enjoy as many seconds of my dream as I could before the coach pulled me off as an imposter. I hid my face behind my hand and ran to the centre of the field. I was so excited, and my heart beat so hard that it hurt my chest. But once in the centre, I froze.

It was so strange standing there with floodlights all around beaming down onto me. The Crystal Stadium was full. The waving crowd surrounded me on all sides, but I couldn't hear them. It was as if my ears didn't work. The kid next to me in red, number 8, was frowning at me, as he didn't know me. He shouted something to me, but I didn't know what. All I could hear was a roaring rush inside my head.

The ref had the whistle in his mouth. I saw that he blew it, but still I heard nothing. I looked around, confused. Number 9, Billy, was screeching at me. He was a tall kid with red hair. He was pointing at my feet. I realised there was a ball there. I tried to move, only I couldn't feel my legs. A kid dressed in West Kingdom blue, number 7, took the ball from me, and raced away toward our goal. That made me so mad. Then it was as if the world made sense again. This wasn't a dream—it was real, and a football match that I had to win.

Pow!

The noise of the cheering crowd suddenly exploded into my head, and it was deafening. I felt power surge through my body like hot fire. Then I knew what I had to do. I forgot everything but football, and I started to run.

I charged back, to help in defence. West Kingdom's best player, blue 7, had the ball. Our midfielder, red 5, tried a good tackle; only blue 7 sidestepped him.

'Hard luck, 5,' I yelled, 'good tackle. Now get back and in line again!'

I was running hard. I was usually the fastest, and I reckoned I could catch blue 7. But, he was already at our last line of defence. Our full back, red 3, charged at him but missed his tackle, and blue 7 ran on. I was racing hard but he was almost at the penalty box. Our goalkeeper slipped on the wet grass, and it was an open goal! West Kingdom couldn't miss. blue 7 drew back his foot to strike.

Wham!

I slid in from the side and kicked the ball away before he could shoot, making sure I didn't foul him. The football rolled out of bounds. The crowd cheered. But the kid took a dive, trying to claim a penalty. Fortunately, the ref had none of it.

'Get up, loser!' Our number 3 yelled at him.

'*Confirming the substitute captain for United Republic is Fritz Best!*' roared the announcer.

The crowd gave a huge cheer. I looked at the overhead screen that zoomed in on me, showing the replay of my tackle, but fortunately, my face had been hidden. By now, the coach would know something was up.

'Nice one, Fritz!' red 4 called over to me. He was far enough away that he couldn't see my face. But I saw that Billy Pace was still staring at me—he knew I wasn't Fritz or Zack. Still he didn't have time to come over, because West Kingdom had a throw-in, close to our goal. I saw the danger straight away.

'Red 2, mark the near post!' I yelled. 'Red 10, cover the cross. And nobody play them onside. Follow my line.'

I took my position in defence. Billy was next to me.

'Who *are* you?' he demanded.

'Zanto. Coach made a change, but they got the name wrong,' I said.

'I'm going to check with him,' he said. But then the throw-in came, and United Republic had to defend. We did well. Our goalkeeper caught the ball from a poor shot, and the crowd cheered.

'Good work boys, well done. Come on, we can get back in this!' I called.

My teammates looked over to me and started smiling

at last. You had to make your team feel good, feel like they could win. And we had to win! For them it was a final, but for me and the Awoken, it was the chance of living again.

The coach was glaring at me hard. He knew I wasn't Zack or Fritz, only he didn't take me off. I kept on running. Our goalkeeper looked up. I whistled and waved and pointed ahead. He saw me and gave a perfect kick. The ball landed just two meters in front of me. I looked up, to see there were eight players between me and West Kingdom's goal—easy odds! I started running, and again I couldn't hear the crowd. It was as if I saw everything in slow motion.

The blue player's foot was trying to nip the ball away—I skipped around him. A sliding tackle came from the side—I jumped over it. There was a wall of defence, three players, but I zigzagged and moved my feet so fast they had no idea which way I was going. I nutmegged the ball through the defender's legs and sidestepped him. I was in the penalty box.

Then there was just one defender left, a huge vicious-looking fullback who must have seventeen at least. He charged towards me and all but pushed me off the ball. It would have been so easy to fall down and get a penalty, but I moved to the side, and instead of pushing me over, the defender's own weight crashed him onto the grass.

I jumped over him and saw the goalkeeper was off his line. I looked down at the ball, kicked it hard underneath, my toe giving it an extra hook. The chip rose high and fast over the goalkeeper who leapt backwards to try to reach it. The ball floated above his hands and then the spin brought it down and into the net—just as I had planned.

Gooooaaaallllaaaa! The crowd went wild.

I ran to the net, grabbed the ball, and raced back to the centre circle. We had to get two more, and there was no time to waste. But before I had gone three metres, the team mobbed me.

'Great goal—brilliant—cool—well done Cap—nice one Fritz—hang on—who are you?'

'He's called Zanto,' Billy said. 'Coach made a switch.'

'Good,' 4 nodded. 'I can't stand that stuck-up fool Zack.'

'Me neither,' 6 said.

'So, what's the plan, Zanto?' 3 asked.

'Get two more goals and win this final,' I said.

'Brilliant! How?'

'Defenders, whatever you do, don't let another goal in. Watch number 7, he'll break from midfield.'

'Yeah, Zack told us to foul him and take him out,' 3 said.

'No! Play clean, because if you get sent off, we've got no chance. Shut down the centre, make him play wide and always keep two players on him. Then get the ball to midfield and up to us strikers, Billy, number 10, and me.'

'Zack said we always have to pass to him, reckoned only he could score,' 10 said.

'No way! I saw you play, you can score, and Billy too. You just have to believe it. We pass to whoever has the best chance of scoring.'

The ref whistled at us to get on.

'Okay, let's get them!' I yelled.

The team ran to their positions, and West Kingdom kicked off.

I saw a chance and charged up the pitch.

Crunch.

I was on the floor rolling in pain, my ankle had been taken out by blue 4, their dirtiest player. I reckoned my game was over.

30

THE CAPTAIN

The coach raced on with the ice spray, which helped a bit. I tested my ankle—it held up.

'Can you play on, son?' he asked.

'Yeah, if you want me to,' I was surprised he didn't order me off.

'Of course, I want you to; you're the best player on this field,' he said. 'What's your name?'

'Zanto Nero.'

'And do you qualify for the United Republic?'

'Yeah, I was born in the Shambles,' I said.

'Good boy! Now sign here as Zanto,' he thrust a clipboard at me, and I signed my name on the team sheet. 'Now the fourth ref thinks you're Fritz Best. I've no idea how he got it so wrong.'

'I told him I was Fritz,' I said. 'I'm an imposter.'

'No, no, shush now—no *imposters* or we'd be disqualified. We clearly told the refs that the sub-number 7 was Zanto Nero. You've been on the team sheet from the start, isn't that right? Not our fault they got it wrong.' He nodded at me.

'I guess so,' I said. I didn't want us disqualified.

'Good, we'll sort out the mistake out later, but first let's get our hands on that Cuppa.'

'Do you still want me to wear Zack's captain's band?'

'The boys are following you, so you're the captain. Now get forward, and remember, their goalkeeper's not so good at free kicks. Oh, and where is Zack?'

'In a wheelie bin under the building,' I told him. 'He's fine.'

'Well, let's just leave him there until the final whistle, shall we?' The coach smiled. 'Now go get 'em, Zanto!' The coach ran off and we played on

The game was frantic from then, both sides charging at each other, taking shots on goal, but either missing or producing great saves. Still, the United Republic were playing much better now, every player wanting to get the ball and run it forward. I kept yelling to them that they could do it. I saw the coach arguing with the fourth official on the sidelines and stabbing his finger at the team sheet. A minute later there was another announcement.

'*Correction. The number 7 substitute in red is Zanto Nero!*' roared the announcer. I got a cheer from the crowd.

We battled on for another quarter hour, but found no way through to goal. Then, I suddenly saw a break. I was on the right wing when I realised the West Kingdom team all expected me to run forward and wide. I made a start in that direction, and three of their players ran to the right to block me. But then I darted to the left, too fast for them to change direction, and shot up the gap in the centre. The crowd went wild. I ran towards the penalty box, only two defenders ahead. I saw out of the corner of my eye, Billy running to the left behind me.

'I'm here, Zanto,' he yelled.

I reached the penalty box. It would have been fun to go for glory with a twenty-five metre kick, so I pulled right, and the two defenders came with me, expecting me to strike. Instead, I passed the ball between them and laid it on for Billy. He volleyed the ball past the keeper. It was brilliant!

Gooooaaaallllaaaa!

The stadium erupted in roars, and we mobbed him.

'Great goal,' I told him.

'Great pass,' he hugged me. I saw a bit of flesh-coloured paint on his red shirt. I looked down at my arm in alarm. Some green skin was showing where the paint had rubbed off because of sweat. It was too early to lose my disguise! I put my arm behind me.

'Let's see if we can hold on, then beat them in extra time,' Billy said. I looked up at the dark ominous rain clouds. I didn't dare wait, because my paint wouldn't last much longer.

'No, we can win this in normal time. Come on, boys,' I said. 'Believe that we can be champions. Let's get that goal!'

'Yeah!' They gave a roar, and we headed back to our positions.

In the last few minutes, we came close, time and again; but we just couldn't get through. They had almost all their players between us and the goal. The full ninety minutes were up, only three minutes of injury time left. There was no time to waste. I charged towards their goal side-stepping the boots and tackles. I was nearly there.

Smash!

I was taken down by a crashing foul, thirty metres out from West Kingdom's goal. The referee awarded a free kick, and their number 3 kicked the ball out of bounds in fury. There was only one minute left.

The ball rolled out to the sideline, and I ran over to fetch it—every second mattered. That's when I saw him, Reygo, picking up the ball. I couldn't believe he was actually there, watching us. I raced up to him.

'You can do it, Zanto,' he said and he threw the ball to me. 'I know you can get the goal—curl it.'

'I will!' I grinned and caught the ball. Knowing that he was watching inspired me. I ran back to the ref and placed the ball down.

Thunder suddenly rumbled above, but thankfully no rain yet. The West Kingdom players stood in a wall in front of the goal.

'You're going to miss, wimp!' blue 4 shouted to me. 'It's too far for you to score.'

Billy was next to me—he was bigger and stronger.

'Do you want me to take the shot?' he asked. 'They won't expect it, and I can reach the goal from here.'

'I know you can, but so can I. I have to do it,' I said. 'So much more depends on it.'

'Okay, score then!' He gave me a thumbs-up.

I stepped five strides back from the ball and two to the left. I couldn't see the goal behind the blue wall, but I knew where it was. This was it, my only chance. I thought of the kids locked up on the Island—I had to get this goal.

I looked only at the ball. I ran in, planted my left leg, held out my left arm for balance, and then swung my right foot as hard as I could across the lower right side of the ball. The wall jumped high as the ball shot to the right of them.

'Ha, you missed, loser!' blue 4 yelled.

But the ball swung back hard and fast left. The goal-keeper dived but too late.

Gooooaaaallllaaaa!

The ref blew the whistle and the final was over. The United Republic had won!

I raced away as the whole stadium went mad screaming. I jumped onto my knees and skidded to a halt in the centre circle, arms raised. The boys chased after me, and then we all collapsed into a massive hug of victory. We stood up to take the cheers of the crowd. I thought my heart would explode with pride. Not only had we had won the Cuppa for our country in front of Il Presido and Reygo, but now I would meet Il Presido and save the Awoken.

I stood up and saw the paint had rubbed off my green knees. It was still too soon. They couldn't know I was a zombie until I got on the stage, or they'd never let me near Il Presido.

'Just a massive grass stain,' I pointed them out to my teammates, but they didn't care. They mobbed me.

31

VICTORY SPEECH

Quickly, a low stage was built in the middle of the pitch. Il Presido was sitting on huge velvet chair at one end, and Reygo stood in the centre. We watched West Kingdom go for their runner-up medals. My heart was still beating hard with excitement. That's when I felt more drops of rain, another shower. I looked up at the black clouds and there was a rumble of thunder. Very soon, everyone in the stadium would know what I was. My stomach cramped with nerves.

The United Republic players started going up onto the stage. The announcer called out their name, and each player got a huge cheer. Reygo shook each one by the hand, said 'well played', and handed them their medals.

Then they walked to Il Presido and gave a bow. Our Great Leader smiled at them and nodded his head.

'No hard feelings for taking your name?' I asked Fritz Best.

'No way, you won the Cuppa,' he slapped my back.

It was my turn to go up.

'Shouldn't we fetch Zack, and let *him* take the Cuppa,' I asked the coach.

'It was you who led the team to victory, not Zack. You deserve it, Zanto,' he said to me.

The rain was getting heavier. I wiped it from my eyes and saw the green skin on my hand where the paint had washed away even more. This was it then. The coach pushed me forward.

'*And here is the substitute captain, Zanto Nero!*' The announcer called out, and the crowd went wild.

'*Zanto—Zanto—Zanto—Zanto—Zanto—Zanto—Zanto—Zanto—Zanto!*'

I walked up to Reygo, my smile so big that I thought my face would split.

'Well done, Zanto. You're a great player and captain,' he said to me. 'I hope to see you at our Youth Academy in Northland one day soon.' He handed me my medal, and I thought my heart would explode with pride. Then I saw that Sally Singson was here. I could tell by the way she looked at me that she knew who I truly was. She thrust the microphone under my nose.

'Say something Zanto—tell the truth,' she whispered to me. 'Now's your chance.'

This was the moment I'd waited for; only now I was scared.

'Errmmm…' I said into the microphone. 'Thanks Reygo, for coming here. It was my greatest dream to meet you. And thanks to the team and Coach for letting me be their captain, when I was only a substitute. And thanks, Your Excellentness, for caring enough about kids to give us the Hope Games.'

Il Presido smiled and nodded, then he stood, picked up the Cuppa, and walked over to me.

'But before I take the Cuppa, I have a confession to make,' I said. This was it—I was going to tell them I was a zombie. I hoped that they wouldn't neutralise me right there. 'I came here tonight, so that I could show you what I truly am, so that I could tell you what is really happening on the Isl…'

But I never got a chance to finish.

'Stop!'

Zack Starr charged onto the stage in his underwear and snatched the Cuppa from his uncle's hands. The crowd gave a massive gasp that echoed around the stadium.

'He's an imposter. *I'm* the captain not him!'

The crowd booed, and Reygo frowned at him. Il Presido looked furious.

'That's enough of your bad behaviour, Zack,' Il Presido said. 'You were substituted for poor play, and Zanto helped the team win. Now step down before I fetch your mother.'

All the boys of the United Republic team cheered and clapped. But Zack wasn't done yet.

'But he wasn't on the team sheet. He's an illegal player, an imposter. And that's not all—he's a *zombie* and a man-eater!' He pointed at me.

'Don't be ridiculous,' Il Presido said. 'Zombies can't play soccer and lead a team. They can't even speak!'

'But look at him; it's true!' Zack screamed. 'He's green! He's a zombie!'

'Don't be a poor loser, Zack. Such pathetic stories won't work. Zanto is clearly...' but Il Presido trailed off as he looked at me. The other boys and the coach were staring at me too, and pulling back, scared.

I looked down. My body paint had completely washed off showing my real skin. I saw my face on the huge screens overhead—green skin, red eyelids, and yellow pointy teeth. The crowd gave another enormous gasp of shock, but Sally smiled at me and nodded. This was the reason I was here.

'Yes, it's true,' I said into the microphone. 'I am a zombie, and I wasn't on the team sheet. I'm an imposter…'

A huge groan echoed through the stadium. The coach threw his file onto the ground in despair.

'We were so close!' he yelled.

'But I'm not a man-eater, and I'm not dangerous!' I continued. 'And I'm not the only one—there are many more zombies like me who would never hurt anyone.'

'He's lying; he is dangerous—he tried to eat me!' Zack yelled. 'Somebody neutralise him.'

The boys stepped back further from me.

'I'm telling the truth, Your Excellentness. I'm a vegetarian.' I turned to Our Great Leader. 'I've never attacked anyone.'

That's when I heard the first screams from the crowd.

'*Zombie attack! Danger!*' came a yell, then another, and another.

'*Evil zombies! They want to kill us!*' The crowd was all roaring in terror and fury.

'*Somebody neutralise them!*'

I felt a heavy sadness as their mistrust and hatred overwhelmed me, like it was sucking all the hope from my heart. I'd failed to convince them. They'd never believe we were still human inside.

'Zanto! Look out!' I heard a call.

Then I saw what the crowd was actually shouting about.

32

DEEZEE ATTACK

This will take too long to tell you, but imagine it all happens in an instant, before anyone had time to react.

I turned and saw Nala and Obi running onto the pitch, chased by a hoard of maddened screeching DeeZees, mouths wide, and yellows fangs dripping under the bright floodlights. I recognised some of them from the Pen, including white-haired Gangster and the Mohican dude. They were all man-eaters! I couldn't understand how they got here; all I knew was that they were hungry and dangerous. Not even a full second after I saw them, the floodlights went out and we were plunged into blackness. There were screams all around the stadium.

'Everyone stay here on the stage,' Il Presido called.

'You'll be hurt running in the dark, and the zombies may reach you. My soldiers will save us.'

There was mayhem all around. But above that noise, I could hear the snarling and smell the DeeZees coming through the dark. Then, with my red night vision, I saw their luminous green skin and the red light of their eyes as they raced towards us through the night. Nala and Obi reached me first. I jumped off the stage to meet them.

'Take this,' Obi threw me a baseball bat. Nala had her pole, and Obi his bare hands. We stood in a row between the rabid zombies and the N-Deds behind us.

'How are they here?' I asked them.

'It was Grimm,' Nala said. 'We saw him release them, but we couldn't stop him.'

'But why?' I asked.

'Talk later,' Obi said. 'It's on!'

The first snarling wave arrived. The DeeZees screeched in our faces, and we screeched back. It was the same as the other times, like a dog and hyena checking each other out, not sure whether we were the same species or not, deciding whether to attack. Then suddenly the floodlights boomed back on, and we were drowned in light. The DeeZees went insane with fury under such a terrible glare hurting their eyes. The DeeZees lunged forward, going for blood.

Whip—whack.

Nala knocked one side-ways and unconscious.

Ker-chow.

Obi flung one back four metres, but he jumped back up and raced forward again.

Pow

I sent the white-haired gangster dude onto his backside. But that only made them madder, and they all attacked again.

Whip-whack-ker-chow whack-ker-chow-pow pow-whip-ker-chow!

We fought them back, waiting for Il Presido's soldiers, but they never came.

'Where are my guards?' I heard Il Presido cry.

'Don't worry, sir,' I yelled. 'We can stop them.'

The DeeZees roared forward once more, desperate to get to the tasty N-Deds.

Whip-whack-ker-chow-whack-ker-chow-pow-pow-whip-ker-chow.

We fought them back once more, only this time Reygo and the two teams joined in, forming a guard to protect Il Presido. They kicked back any DeeZees who made it through. The only one who stayed cowering on the stage was Zack.

'I'm not liking this guy,' Reygo said, with a glance in Zack's direction.

By then most of the zombies were knocked out on the ground. But some just wouldn't give up. White-haired Gangster nearly reached Il Presido.

Obi raced over, picked him up, and flung him down the pitch a few metres. He didn't get up that time.

'Arrgg!' Obi roared with triumph, showing off his green muscles, and his yellow-fanged smile beamed on the overhead screens. The last three DeeZees standing attacked.

Whip-whack-crack!

Nala took them out on her own, then stood in ultimate warrior pose, her pole hooked under her arm.

'Wow!' I heard Billy say next to me. 'She is one cool zombie-chick!' He was right—she looked powerful!

Everything went very quiet. I looked around. There was still no sign of Il Presido's soldiers, but we seemed to have kept him safe. All the DeeZees looked out for the count. I picked up the football we'd won the match with.

'Nnaaarggg!' Mohican zombie suddenly jumped up and charged towards me. I didn't have time to fight him off.

Bham!

There was an orange and green flash before my eyes, and the DeeZee was knocked out cold. I looked up to see G-Nut next to me, a massive grin on his green face.

'Nice one,' I laughed.

'Didn't think you were going to get all the glory, did you, Zero? I decided mates had to stick together. I jumped over the turnstiles when they weren't looking.'

'Brilliant!' I high fived him.

And then the boys from the team mobbed me, just like we'd won the Cuppa again! I heard the crowd erupting all around in cheers once more.

'*Zanto-Zanto-Zanto-Zanto-Zanto-Zanto-Zanto-Zanto-Zanto!*'

Obi, Nala, G-Nut, and I stood there in the middle of the pitch, green zombies, and listened as the whole stadium of N-Deds applauded us. I was grinning so hard it hurt. It seemed like zombies could be heroes after all. It meant even more than winning the Cuppa. We had shown the world we were just normal kids on the inside and nothing to be afraid of.

It was then that Il Presido's armed soldiers raced onto the pitch.

'Never fear, Your Excellency!' the commanding officer called. 'We're here to protect you!'

They surrounded and pointed their guns at us. We stepped closer together.

'Hey, Zanto hasn't done anything wrong! He saved Il Presido's life!' Billy cried. He and the other footballers ran to stand between us and the solders. I felt so proud.

'You're too late! Where have you been?' Il Presido roared at his guard.

'We were called to an emergency, a zombie attack outside the grounds, only no one was there,' the officer stammered.

'Because the zombies were attacking us in here, you fools!' Il Presido yelled. 'And *those* kids aren't the danger. Put your guns down!'

'Yes Excellency,' they lowered their guns.

'But what shall we do with these dreadful zombies?' The officer pointed to us.

'Don't worry about them, just get those dangerous ones locked up safe before they wake up again,' Il Presido ordered.

'Yes, Excellency; sorry, Excellency,' the officer bowed low.

Il Presido waved him away in annoyance then came towards us.

'It seems you are most remarkable, zombie children,' he said to us. 'How can you speak, and think? Why do you not attack like the others?'

Everything we did and said was played to the whole stadium on the big screens.

'It's because we are *Awoken*, Your Excellentness,' I told him. 'We came back to life again. We might be green, but otherwise we're just the same as any other kids,' I said. 'And we need your help, because we just want to live real lives again. We want a future and dreams, just like normal kids. And so do all the other Awoken kids locked up on the Island. They all want to be free.'

Il Presido was listening to me, and it looked like he truly cared.

'This is Nala; she's so smart, and she wants to be a doctor,' I said. 'Only she's got no books.'

Nala's face came on the big screen. She stared at Il Presido, and she looked like she was busting with brains.

'I want to go to school, then college,' she told him.

Il Presido nodded.

'And this is Obi. He's really brave,' I said. 'He wants to be in the Special Forces. He'd make a better guard for you than your soldiers,' I said.

The soldiers glared at me, but I didn't care. Obi nodded, still keeping his eye on the DeeZees.

'And I want to moon-dance!' G-Nut yelled.

'I see…' Il Presido frowned a bit at that. 'But what about you, Zanto?' he asked me. 'What do you want to do?'

'Find my dad,' I said. 'Oh, and play for Real Magique.'

Reygo smiled and gave a thumb's up, and that was worth more than a million dollars.

'But it's not just us,' I carried on. 'The Island is full of kids who are Awoken. They all need your help. They could all have a future only…'

I stopped in shock. I was about to say how terrible Capo Grey was when the man himself turned up, sweating in his grey suit.

33

Z FOR Z51?

Capo Grey climbed into the stage.

'Apologies Excellency,' he said. 'I must take full responsibility. These dangerous zombie children escaped from the Island and must be returned immediately.'

Il Presido glared at him.

'It seems I am surrounded by buffoons,' he said. 'A Presidential Guard who isn't here to save my life, and a prison governor who lets all his zombies escape.' He pointed at the unconscious DeeZees.

'Your Excellency...' Capo Grey pointed at the DeeZees. '*Those* creatures are not my responsibility. They were taken from the Island on army orders. It is the army who let them escape.'

'He's lying!' Nala said. 'We saw his guard, Grimm,

letting them out of the cage just now.'

The crowd muttered, angry.

'Nonsense and lies,' Capo Grey laughed at her. 'You see, Il Presido, these Awoken zombies have devious brains and are capable of making up stories. They can't be controlled like the dead ones, which makes them more dangerous. For everyone's safety, they need to be kept on the Island. They have everything they need there, and are free to roam around.'

'He's lying again,' Sally Singson stepped up with her microphone. 'The children are telling the truth. I've seen the camp on the Island and they have no freedom, or books. Capo Grey warned me to keep quiet.'

The crowd was angry again. Capo Grey glared at Sally. Il Presido looked concerned now. He was going to help us for sure.

'Sir, I see that your good heart would like to help these young zombies, but they have entered the Third State, against your command, and are criminals,' Capo Grey spoke up again. 'Z51 must be returned to the Island, *for the greater good!*'

The way Capo Grey spoke made me feel like he was speaking in code to Our Great Leader.

'This is *Z51*?' Il Presido stared at me, like he saw me for the first time.

'I'm not *Z51*—I'm Zanto Nero!' I cried. 'I'm not devious or dangerous. I just want to play football. Please don't send us back to the Island because then we'll have no hope, and our hearts will stop again. Please Excellentness, we just want to have a home, and a life like all the kids here.'

'But *Z51*, the Island *is* your home now,' Capo Grey spoke in his soothing soft voice that I hated. 'You are orphans. I just want to take care of you. Who'll look after you, if I don't? No one on the Mainland will have a zombie under their roof. You can't be trusted.'

Il Presido looked like he believed what Capo Grey was saying.

'I'm sorry, Z51,' Our Great Leader said at last. 'I must always act for the greater good.'

I wasn't Zanto any more—I was Z51 again.

'What about *our* greater good?' Nala cried. 'Capo Grey just wants Zanto's blood to experiment with. He wants to kill us all!'

Capo Grey grabbed at Nala, but Ginga-Nut and Obi jumped in front of him. Obi snarled, his fangs bared, and Nala had her stick ready to attack. Everything had gone so wrong.

'Step down, or I shall have the Guard restrain you!' Il Presido roared at us.

We all stepped back.

'I'm sorry, Z51. If I had another choice I promise I would take it,' he continued. 'You and your friends are brave, but you must return to the Island. There's no other place for orphan zombies.'

Zack grinned at me evilly, but the players on both teams started to complain, and Reygo shook his head. Some of the crowd started to boo. I didn't know how to argue against Capo Grey. What other choice could we offer Il Presido?

'Zanto... Zanto... Zanto... Zanto!'

I thought I heard someone calling my name, but I couldn't see who.

'Zanto... Zanto... Zanto!'

Someone was definitely calling me. Everyone around me could hear it too. There was a bit of commotion in the crowd nearby.

'Zanto... Zanto!'

I saw a figure climb over the barrier and start running across the pitch. It was a man, not too tall, and with a limp that looked so familiar, like he had pain in his knees because of all the hours he spent bending and squatting, weeding, and planting rich people's gardens. Still, I didn't dare believe it. He came closer.

'Zanto!'

And then I knew it was true.

'Dad!'

He reached the stage and picked me up in a massive hug!

'I knew that if you'd escaped the bomb, nothing would stop you being here to meet your idol, Reygo!' Dad cried.

I couldn't answer him because I was sure I'd cry, and no way was that happening. I just hugged him tight, feeling safe for the first time in a year.

'I'm sorry I didn't see your goals. I couldn't get away from work,' Dad said. 'But I heard them on the radio. I just had to see with my own eyes that it was really you.'

'It's me, Dad,' I said but then looked down, suddenly ashamed. 'Only I'm not me anymore. I died Dad—I'm a zombie now...'

'And I've never been prouder of my son,' Dad said.

Like I told you before. My dad always knows what to say.

He pushed me behind him and spoke to Capo Grey.

'I heard your words, sir,' he said, standing straight despite his sore knees. 'I can assure you that my son is no orphan, and his friends will be welcome under *my* roof.'

Nala, G-Nut, and Obi moved next to me, behind Dad. He had that effect on everyone, made them feel safe. Sally Singson held her microphone out, and Dad took it. He spoke to Il Presido like he talked to Our Great Leader every day.

'Your Excellency, these children are no danger to anyone. Surely, you won't send them back to prison on the Island? I trust in your merciful good heart.'

Some of the crowd clapped.

'That man is an illegal immigrant from the Shambles, Excellency,' Capo Grey cried. 'He should be in jail himself!'

The crowd hissed. I looked at Dad, scared for him, but he was calm.

'Not true, Your Excellency,' he said and took some papers out of his pocket. He handed them to Il Presido. 'Here is my visa issued before the Infection. I have every right to be in the Third State, and to have my son with me. I ask you and the good people of United Republic...' he turned to the television camera and spoke to the crowd directly, his face on the big screen.

'These are the *Hope Games*. Do you want these heroic children who saved Il Presido's life to be allowed a good life with a loving and settled family, or to be sent back to a prison with no chance of release, and no future? What is actually for the greater good? Hope or despair?'

'*Hope-hope-hope!*' The crowd chanted.

Dad then drew me and Nala under his arms, and Obi and G-Nut stood behind us.

'They are all my children now, until they find their parents,' he said.

Capo Grey glared but said nothing. Il Presido held up his hand, and the crowd went silent.

'Mr Nero has every right to be in the Capital,' Il

Presido announced and handed Dad's papers back. The crowd cheered. 'And to these Awoken Zombie Children, I say...'

We all waited.

'Thank you for your bravery. Go home with Mr Nero. And may your dreams come true.'

The stadium went wild with cheering. The boys from both teams clapped, and Reygo gave me a high five!

'And what about the other Awoken kids on the Island? Can they go free too?' I asked.

'I shall consider it,' Il Presido said. 'Come and see me at the Palace next week, and I'll decide the way forward.'

He smiled, and Capo Grey scowled. That gave me hope.

It was time for us to go.

'Good luck, Zanto,' Reygo shook my hand. Then, best of all, he gave me a signed number 7 shirt. It was the best day of my life! Nala, Obi, G-Nut, and I walked off the pitch with Dad to the sound of claps and cheers. As we reached the edge of the grass, I looked back.

Capo Grey and Il Presido were talking together, seriously. It didn't look like the prison governor was in trouble. Then Il Presido stared at me. I didn't know what his expression meant, but it made me feel uncomfortable. I was worried that Capo Grey was telling him lies about me and that he might believe them. But then I remembered to be happy, because my dad was here.

'Come on then, kids,' Dad laughed. 'I guess even zombies like ice cream? I'll get you some on the way home.'

That cheered me up right away. And I totally forgot to worry about what might happen next. Because hey, I'd just won the Cuppa for The United Republic (well until we were disqualified because I was an imposter), met Reygo, and shown the world I was just like them. And best of all, I'd found my dad again.

Was Z still for Zero, for Z51? No way. Z was for Zanto!

THE FUTURE

That's my story so far. I don't know how it ends yet, because I still have my second life to live. I'm so excited about seeing Dad's place and making a new home. Will people actually accept us Awoken kids living in their neighbourhood? I hope so, but then how would I have felt a year ago if my neighbour was suddenly a green zombie? Guess we'll just have to see how it goes. At least Nala, Obi, and Ginga-Nut will be with me; they're brave enough to face anything and will stand by me.

But there's still stuff I don't understand. Like why did Grimm set off a zombie invasion into the stadium? And did Capo Grey know about it? I reckon he did, because Grimm never did anything without his boss telling him. But why? Nala thinks that it was to frighten Il Presido and convince him how dangerous zombie kids could be.

Perhaps then, he'd agree to neutralise us all, like Capo Grey wanted.

I don't know if that's true, I hope not. Still something worries me. Once Il Presido knew I was Z51, his face changed, and he said that I should be back in prison. The only reason Capo Grey wanted me there was for my mutated blood, to use as a lethal weapon in the fight against zombies. I can't think badly of Our Great Leader, but I don't trust Capo Grey. Perhaps he'd convinced Il Presido that I was dangerous. I just can't forget the way they both stared at us as we left the stadium. Still, I'm going to the Palace next week, and at least then, I'll be able to tell Il Presido what's truly happening to the kids on the Island, without Capo Grey to interfere.

But hey, whatever happens in the future, today is the best day of my life. I'm with Dad again, walking with his hand on my shoulder. Dad says our home is very small and poor, even more so than the one in the Shambles. But it can't be that bad if I'm with him, because I know he'll make it good. No matter how poor we are.

I haven't told him about Romeo yet, and I'm dreading it. Still, I'm happier than I could ever have imagined I would be since I died. So here I am, in a new city, having to start a new life again. I admit I'm scared, but it's better than being locked up on the Island. I have hope now. And I have a new massive dream too...

I'm going to be the first zombie to play for Real Magique!

Jayne Lyons is an internationally published, award winning children's author. If you enjoyed *Z for Zanto*, you'll love her other books, *100% Wolf* and *100% Hero*. Also, watch out for the *100% Wolf* animated feature film to be released in 2020 by Flying Bark Productions!

You can find more information on Jayne's website. www.jaynelyons.com

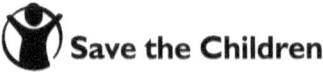 **Save the Children**

To find out more about the work *Save the Children* does to support children in Australia and around the world, visit the 'Our Stories' section on our website at www.savethechildren.org.au/Our-Stories